PENGUIN (Penguin logo) CLASSICS

SIR GAWAIN AND THE GREEN KNIGHT

ADVISORY EDITOR: BETTY RADICE

BRIAN STONE wrote his first book, *Prisoner from Alamein*, which had a foreword by Desmond MacCarthy, in 1944. After the war, during which he was decorated, he entered the teaching profession and taught English in boys' schools for eleven years. He then trained teachers for ten years at Loughborough and Brighton. In 1969 he became a founder member of the Open University, where he was Reader in English Literature for the rest of his professional life. He has four other verse translations to his credit in the Penguin Classics: modern English renderings of *Medieval English Verse*; *The Owl and the Nightingale, Cleanness, St Erkenwald*; *King Arthur's Death: Morte Arthure, Le Morte Arthur*; and Chaucer's *Love Visions*. He also published critical studies of Chaucer and Keats in the Penguin Critical Studies series.

Brian Stone died in London in March 1995. In its obituary the *Independent* described him as 'a brilliant teacher, an enthusiast for good English and an exceptionally brave man. He was unmistakable with his jaunty, determined, one-legged walk and air of buoyant optimism.'

SIR GAWAIN AND THE GREEN KNIGHT

SECOND EDITION

TRANSLATED
WITH AN INTRODUCTION BY
BRIAN STONE

PENGUIN BOOKS

PENGUIN BOOKS

Published by the Penguin Group
Penguin Books Ltd, 80 Strand, London WC2R 0RL, England
Penguin Putnam Inc., 375 Hudson Street, New York, New York 10014, USA
Penguin Books Australia Ltd, 250 Camberwell Road, Camberwell, Victoria 3124, Australia
Penguin Books Canada Ltd, 10 Alcorn Avenue, Toronto, Ontario, Canada M4V 3B2
Penguin Books India (P) Ltd, 11 Community Centre, Panchsheel Park, New Delhi – 110 017, India
Penguin Books (NZ) Ltd, Cnr Rosedale and Airborne Roads, Albany, Auckland, New Zealand
Penguin Books (South Africa) (Pty) Ltd, 24 Sturdee Avenue, Rosebank 2196, South Africa

Penguin Books Ltd, Registered Offices: 80 Strand, London WC2R 0RL, England

www.penguin.com

This translation first published 1959
Second edition 1974
51

Copyright © Brian Stone, 1959, 1964, 1974
All rights reserved

Printed in England by Clays Ltd, St Ives plc
Set in Monotype Bembo

ISBN-13: 978–0–14–044092–8

Contents

Preface to the Second Edition

SINCE the Penguin Classic *Sir Gawain and the Green Knight* was first published in 1959, much critical work has been done on the poem, and two more important editions of it have appeared. Also, in the fourteen years since its first appearance, the book has been widely used in schools, colleges and universities. It therefore seemed right to revise the whole work in the hope that it would better fulfil the purposes for which it was being used. Since a work of translation in verse stands or falls by its accuracy and by its quality as poetry, I have completely re-worked the translation, benefiting both from the comments of critics, among whom I should like chiefly to acknowledge A. C. Spearing, and from my own experience in having, since 1959, translated all the other poems in the group. It is for the reader to say how good this new version is: all I can say is that it is truer to the original word and thought order, more accurate in meaning, and more concrete in expression than the 1959 version.

As for the support material, I have adopted a threefold approach to the poem to replace the single approach of the first edition. Then, the general reader only was considered. In the present edition the introduction is still mainly addressed to him, and the background about Arthurian and other cultural material which figures in the appendixes is slightly reduced in quantity and importance and conflated into a single section. The two new features, which are intended to be useful to students as well as to the general reader, are the notes, and the essays which follow the poem. The lines to which the notes refer are marked with asterisks in the text and the notes themselves appear at the end of the book. These notes are more than footnotes: they deal with problems of translation and matters of critical interest as well as explanation of detail, and are designed as an apparatus to lead the reader, as he proceeds, into interesting complexities and problem areas as they arise. In the two essays following the poem, by examining the Green Knight and all he stands for and works by, and by assessing the character of Gawain as it unfolds in the action, I record what the poem means to me. The third essay is on the Christmas 1971 production at the University Theatre, Newcastle of Peter Stevens's selection from this text. I hope the foregoing will explain why in the following pages I have sometimes worked over an aspect of the poem more than once in slightly differing and not necessarily complementary ways. The bibliography has been deliberately limited and explained so as to be useful to students.

I should like to express my thanks to the following: Dr Marlene Spiegler of Columbia University, for bringing up to date and letting me use her complete *Sir Gawain and the Green Knight* bibliography; Mr J. Trapp, Librarian of the Warburg Institute, the University of London, for many valuable suggestions about the translation made when I was revising it for inclusion in an Oxford University Press anthology of English literature to appear in the United States in 1973, of which he is the medieval editor; and Oren Stone, for his detailed commentary on my first edition translation, in the light of Davis, Waldron and Gollancz.

Lastly, I should like to acknowledge my dependence on the three scholarly editions of the poem, and consequently my indebtedness to: Norman Davis (the editor of the Second Edition of J. R. R. Tolkien and E. V. Gordon's well-known edition of the poem – first edition 1925, second edition 1967, Oxford); R. A. Waldron (editor of the York Medieval Texts edition of the poem, Arnold 1970); and to the Oxford University Press, who in 1959 gave me permission to use material in the notes to the edition of the poem by Sir Israel Gollancz and Dr Mabel Day, published in 1940 for the Early English Text Society, and to quote three stanzas of Gollancz's text. For this, see page 156/8. For this second edition, I have worked closely with all three editions. Wherever in the text I have cited them, I have referred to them simply by the name of the editor – Davis, or Waldron, or Gollancz.

Introduction

IN English fourteenth-century literature, alongside the work of Chaucer, with his mastery of the forms, techniques and subject matter of contemporary Italian and French poetry, all duly transmuted in English language and ways of thought, there stands a body of alliterative poetry which reflects a different tradition with its own equally assured masteries. We cannot say for certain whether the tradition of alliterative poetry had been continuously fostered since its heyday in the centuries before the Norman Conquest, because the poetry which has survived neither represents the various intervening periods nor shows a steady line of development. All we can be sure of is that at the very time when Chaucer was flourishing, poets of the west and north-west of England were producing a number of fine long poems in alliterative verse, of which *Sir Gawain and the Green Knight* is the pearl.

These poets wrote in a verse which was slightly looser than the tight alliterative form favoured by the Anglo-Saxon epic poets. Their basic line is one of four stresses, three of which begin with either the same consonant, or any vowel (a stressed initial vowel is vocally but not alphabetically preceded by an unvarying glottal stop, which gives the same alliterative effect as a consonant when repeated), with a caesura after two stresses. The first half of the line generally carries the main weight of the meaning, and a common variant is to have a third alliterating stress-word in it. There are usually one or two unstressed syllables between stress-words, occasionally none or three; and the alliterative pattern of the line is sometimes reduced to a pair of stress-words, placed either at the beginning of each half-line, or in the middle of the line. In the translation, although I have generally been faithful to the form, there are on the whole more unstressed syllables, and that is because our language has more of them than Middle English.

The technical demands of the verse seem to be reflected in the characteristics of the language used: stock alliterative phrases abound and, as Marie Boroff (Bibliography 1, pp. 45-76) has shown in connection with *Sir Gawain and the Green Knight*, many of the words in the poem which were already poetic and archaic in the fourteenth century occur often in the alliterating position. To give some idea of this language, I append, beginning on page 156, three stanzas of the original poem.

Together with their chosen form, the alliterative poets kept the distinctive qualities of the northern ethos: the stark realism of Norse and Anglo-Saxon literature, its harsh natural setting, its frequent combination of violent event, laconic understatement and grim humour, its continuous strength and moral seriousness. But they also freely absorbed the new southern elements. In form, they recognized Romance prosody, sometimes grouping alliterative lines in stanzas, whether rhymed or unrhymed, and often adding, as in our poem, rhymed quatrains which impose periods on the flow of standard alliterative verse. And in subject matter and tone they showed themselves capable of absorbing the entire Romance scheme of things, including the whole apparatus of chivalric courts and courtly love.

The fusion of these elements gives *Sir Gawain and the Green Knight* its extraordinary richness. Beside the refined, almost Greek, simplicity of Chaucer's poetry, the ornamented verse of the contemporary north-western poet rears like a Hindu temple, exotic and densely fashioned. Its outlandish quality derives partly from its language, which contains many hard-sounding words of Norse origin which are rare or non-existent in Chaucer, and partly from its expression of an early medieval northern culture which was to be largely submerged in a rival culture, the one based on the London-Oxford-Cambridge triangle and destined to become ours. But exotic though it may be, there is nothing sprawling or inorganic about the poem, although the genre of Romance has produced some of the least shapely works in literature. At a perfect moment in English literary development, when the spirit of the Middle Ages is fully alive but has not long to last, the poet has evoked the heroic atmosphere of saga, with its grim deeds and threatening landscapes; has absorbed into traditional English form the best of the finesse and spirit of French romance; has used in subtle transmutation pagan folk material drawn mostly from the early Celtic tradition; and thrown over all his elements the shimmering grace of his Christian consciousness. The result is a Romance both magical and human, powerful in dramatic incident, and full of descriptive and philosophic beauty; in which wit, irony and occasional pathos provide constant enrichment, so that when the dénouement with its profound moral comes, it is not felt merely as didactic, but as the climax of a work which has for subject the celebration of abounding civilized life, with all its ambiguities and special preserves of fine feeling.

The events in the poem are as follows:

FIT I. During the revelry at King Arthur's Court one new year, the Green Knight rides in with an axe, and challenges anyone present to strike him a blow with it, provided he can give a return blow a year later. Gawain, the king's nephew, takes up the challenge and cuts off the visitor's head. The body, still living, picks up the head, which tells Gawain to look for him at the Green Chapel in a twelvemonth's time. The visitor leaves.

FIT II. Ten months later, Gawain rides north looking for the Green Chapel. On Christmas Eve he comes to a castle, whose lord invites him to stay for Christmas and New Year, since the Green Chapel is nearby. He proposes that Gawain should rest during the intervening days, entertained by his wife, while he goes hunting, and that at the end of each day they should exchange whatever they had gained.

FIT III. Successive hunts, of deer, boar, and fox, take place while the host's wife, in three visits to Gawain's bedroom, attempts his chastity, but gains no more than kisses, which Gawain duly gives to his host at the end of each day, in exchange for the trophies of the hunt.

But during the third interview the Lady, after giving up the attempt to seduce Gawain, persuades him to accept her girdle, which she says will protect his life: Gawain conceals the gift from the lord.

FIT IV. Led by a guide, Gawain goes to the Green Chapel, where the Green Knight gives him three feinted blows, just nicking his neck with the third stroke. He then explains that he is Gawain's host, that the first two feinted blows were for the two occasions on which Gawain faithfully gave him his gains, the wife's kisses, and that the nick was a reproof for Gawain's failure to reveal the gift of the girdle. Gawain laments his fault, leaves the Green Knight, and goes back to court, where, after hearing his story, his peers judge that he has brought honour to the Round Table.

When the probable sources* of the different parts of the poem, and the way they are used in combination and transmutation, are examined, it becomes clear that the poet has a wholly original conception which owes little to any other work we know of. The earliest source of the poem's main plot, that concerning the Beheading Game, appears to have been the eighth- or ninth-century Irish epic of *Fled Bricrend* or *Bricriu's Feast*, in one episode of which Cuchulain agrees to play the game with Uath mac Imomain (Terror, son of Great Fear): Cuchulain strikes off Uath's head, and when he comes back next day to offer his own head, Uath aims three blows without hurting him and declares him a champion. Uath is a savage churl, the Irish for which is *bachlach*, and it is suggested that the name of the lord of the castle in *Sir Gawain and the Green Knight*, which is Sir Bertilak, derives from this word. The Beheading Game appears elsewhere in folklore and medieval romance: Larry D. Benson (Bibliography 2, p. 2) considers that 'the principal and direct source of the beheading episode in Sir Gawain is *Le Livre de Caradoc*', a twelfth- or thirteenth-century French romance of courtly character in which 'Arthur and his fame are the centre of attention' (p. 3). Among many parallels that Benson cites are: Guinevere's involvement, the young knight's extraordinary

*For further discussion of parallel stories and possible sources, see Davis pp. xv–xx.

humility (in *Caradoc* he has been knighted only the day before), and the antagonist's similarity in all sorts of ways. He wears green, and has 'something of the same combination of merriment, beauty and menace that characterizes the Green Knight' (p. 3).

The second main component theme, that of the Temptation by the Hostess, is a common one, and in the analogues, among which probably the Anglo-Norman *Yder* is the closest, the essential point is that it is the wife of the Host who tries to seduce the guest in order that the husband may have power over him. The Temptation theme is expressed as part of the Exchange of Winnings game, in which the Host promises Gawain all his gains on the hunting field in return for Gawain's gains while he is resting in the castle. Since the Beheading Game is also based on a promise of a fair exchange (though no spook who can survive decapitation would be thought fair by his adversary!), and fair exchanges depend on troth-plighters keeping their word, the framework of the whole poem thus becomes a game of truth. The combination of the three elements described has no parallel in medieval literature. To bind them all in moral as well as narrative significance, the poet provides two important emblems which he uses as touchstones for his hero and reminders to the reader at key points in the game: Gawain's shield with its pentangle, the emblem of his knightly virtue, and the Hostess's green girdle, the emblem of his fault. All in all, the grand design, no less than the beauty and organic variety of the parts, proclaims the poet a genius of a kind without parallel in early English literature.

All readers and critics of *Sir Gawain* have to make up their minds how much pagan ritual material survives from the sources, and what use the poet makes of it; and this is a real problem. On both sides of the shadowy frontier which fails to divide pagan myth from medieval Christianity, the land has, through the centuries, been largely claimed by the Church. Modern anthropology has steadily reduced the extent of the land claimed, and some critics have been at pains to interpret the Romances, and among them *Sir Gawain*, in terms of pagan ritual in spite of the often declared Christian purpose of the writers. It is easy to say that both sides are right, but they are, if one accepts Hugh Ross Williamson's argument in *The Arrow and the Sword*: that it is no disservice to the Church to draw attention to the influence of primitive religion on Christianity. Such exposures are in harmony with the idea of progressive revelation. To put it quite straightforwardly, the Crucifixion and the Resurrection gain in force and meaning from the persistence, in pre-Christian myth, of the idea of the slain and resurrected god; the authenticity of *Sir Gawain and the Green Knight* as a medieval Christian poem is not in doubt merely because Gawain is ostensibly the same knight who was the original Grail hero of an earlier literature, a literature which Jessie Weston (Bibliography 3) argues convincingly is based on pagan ritual. Those who have been 'bitten by the Golden Bow-wow', as a mordant phrase has it, think there is a ritual plan underlying *Sir Gawain* which is like that of the primitive quest of the Grail: there is a waste land, to restore the fertility of which a god has to be sacrificed and resurrected. But if such an idea was in the poet's mind, he transmuted it strangely, because in his poem nobody dies or is resurrected either literally or metaphorically, and the state of the land is significant only because it is architectonically related to the events of the poem and the time of the year in which they happen. It is a cold forbidding place in the grip of two successive North European winters. But the Green Knight, whom I discuss on pages 116–28, clearly has some of the pagan attributes of stock figures from primitive folklore. The antagonist of a Christian knight is the right person to have them: it would be a muddled medieval poet who, working in the late fourteenth century and at the level of sophistication which this poet evinces, allowed the Christian Knight to have them as well.

As for Gawain himself, he is the hero whose good faith is on trial from the moment he appears. Since for real understanding of the poem it is important for the reader to consider the detail of Gawain's predicaments and behaviour through medieval eyes, on pages 129–37 I have gone at some length into what his 'good faith' is and into the nature of his shortcoming. His failing is so slight, and he behaves so nearly like a paragon throughout, that the poem becomes a celebration of Christian knightly virtue.

As such, it honours the House of Arthur, of which Gawain is a member, and the Britain which counted Arthur as its tutelary national hero; and above all it is a Christian festival poem. It extols the temporal and spiritual joys of the season as well as the society which expressed them – the aristocratic castle-dwelling community which was conventionally thought to uphold all good order and virtue against the disorder threatening from outside. Within, nobility and all its virtues, rule and Christianity; outside, churlishness and all its vices, misrule and malevolent supernatural forces. But, in the spirit of Christmas, all the events, and especially the plots against Gawain's chastity and life, are presented as a kind of game, with its carefully stated rules and observances and its appropriate audiences. This technique first adumbrates and then makes concrete the poet's didactic scheme, in parallel with the process by which he establishes his equally concrete realm of romance by showing that famous world in incessant vigorous and beautiful action: colourful courts at celebration, tournament or prayer, teeming hunts, dangerous journeys, desolate landscapes under snow or mist or sunshine. But the contest between Gawain and the Green Knight's manifold forces remains always in the foreground.

When the contest is finally decided at the Green Chapel the meaning of the didactic scheme is made plain, and readers who expect a grand romantic finale are disappointed. For here the poet declares the whole point of his Romance. He explains the machinery of magic which has enabled him to focus with finesse on his own moral vision and the hero through whom he communicates it: and he offers, in the atmosphere of lowered tension brought about by the certainty of Gawain's safety, when the cultivated people for whom the poem was written had stilled their heart-beats and could free their minds to receive the lesson, a decorous ending; the hero, after coming through almost incredibly hard tests of his loyalty and good faith, failed the last test because he loved life. That is a failing which, like the members of

King Arthur's court, we understand and condone; more, we rejoice in it, because not to do so would be to affirm death rather than life. It is not just that the poem reflects the perennial 'conflict between ideal codes and human limitations' (Benson, bibliography 4, p. 248): Gawain cannot know that he is in the hands of a just testing apparatus, and must behave as if fighting for his life against a malignant supernatural agency. Counter-charm for charm's the word.

The pattern of the poem shows a most harmonious balance, sometimes between contrasts and sometimes between correspondences. Thus all is warm and Christian where the courtly writ runs, as at Camelot, but the north, where Gawain goes for his ordeal, is cold and mysterious. Yet the northern castle, if it is effectively to play its role in the temptation of Gawain, must be a simulacrum of Arthur's. Hence, since it is the scene of the struggle for Gawain's good faith, the impression it leaves on the reader's mind is more powerful than that left by Camelot, whose splendours may be taken for granted because they are recounted in many a romance. Bertilak's castle, accordingly, when Gawain first saw it, 'shimmered and shone through the shining oaks', although a moment before, in the same wood, the knight was aware of the miserable birds that 'piteously piped away, pinched with cold'. And when Sir Gawain left the castle on his quest for the Green Chapel, he was barely off the end of the drawbridge before he 'climbed by cliffs where the cold clung'.

That the poet is deliberately making patterns, and not merely following the rhythm of his narrative, appears from other parallel episodes and descriptions. Thus, before Gawain sets out from Camelot, there is an elaborate description of his arming and of his shield (ll. 563–669); and when he sets out for the Green Chapel, his arming and the green girdle are described (ll. 2011–62). Then, his journey to the castle (ll. 670–762) is paralleled by his journey to the Green Chapel (ll. 2069–2159); and the description of the northern castle (ll. 764–802) is paralleled by the description of the Green Chapel (ll. 2170–92), both being places where he is to undergo moral ordeals.

The long third fit, which deals with the three hunts and the Lady's three attempts to seduce Gawain, shows the most remarkable pattern-ing of all. Only here does the poet use the medieval narrative tech-nique of 'interlace',* moving from hunt to bed and back again in order to keep parallel processes in focus together. The details of the various hunts are exactly according to hunting usage as laid down in the oldest hunting treatise in English (*The Master of Game*, which was written by Edward Duke of York, early in the fifteenth century), yet the poet has so selected from and worked on his material that each hunt is an allegory-like guide of a parallel stage of the Lady's attempt to seduce Gawain. Thus the account of the first hunt opens with the terror-stricken deer darting down to the dales at the din of hound and horn; and in the bedroom, Gawain is in trepidation at the suddenness and unexpectedness of the Lady's proposition. The second hunt, in which the quarry is 'a baneful boar of unbelievable size', provides the fiercest encounter for Bertilak and his men, and it is Gawain's second visit from the Lady that drives him to almost desperate verbal shifts in order to maintain his courtesy without losing his chastity. This time his very chivalry is called in question. And in the third hunt it is the wily fox that is the victim. The pursuit is all twists and turns, just like the last bedside conversations between the Lady and Gawain. At one point, fox and knight seem like to have escaped, but the fox, having eluded the main hue and cry, lights unluckily on a dog-base, and Gawain, having finally turned the Lady's love-longing into apparent grief for unrequited love, falls into the error of accepting from her a talisman. Bertilak's disgust with the fox's skin parallels the savour of Gawain's little deception in concealing the gift of the girdle.

As to the further significance of the hunts, I do think that there is value in the suggestion of D. W. Robertson Jr. that the three victims, deer, boar and fox, may carry their traditional religious symbolism and may therefore represent respectively the Flesh, the Devil and the World. What is certain is that in medieval iconography as represented in sculpture and illuminated manuscripts, these animals with their

---

*I derive the term, which in fact applies strictly to medieval art, from Eugene Vinaver's *The Rise of Romance* (O.U.P., 1971, pp. 68–98).

associated values are so common that no reasonably educated medieval person could meet them in a story without being aware of what they stood for. Even in a little church not five miles from where I am sitting, there is a thirteenth-century font with a panel on which is sculptured in low-relief the diabolical boar trying to uproot the True Vine with his snout. But there is danger in reading anything too precise into the parallels between the hunting and courtly encounters: successful allegory depends on every component of the story or other artefact having a clear interpretation which contributes to the whole meaning. Here it seems to me that the parallels are mainly of atmosphere and general meaning: there is little profit in attempting absolutely to identify Sir Gawain with hunter or hunted in any episode.

As for the composite figure of the Green Knight/Sir Bertilak, his two selves correspond wonderfully, but such is the poet's skill that the reader not in possession of the final clue can no more than guess at the significance of the correspondences. There are physical resemblances, but the full-blooded, lofty courtesy of the knightly self and the fierce uncouthness of the supernatural being come only afterwards to be seen as 'blossoms upon one tree'. The high moment when the Green Knight waves his beard before Arthur's court, in a stillness so intense that all hear him clear his throat, matches in splendour the moment when the Host and the boar plunge into the stream together, the boar dead, the man exulting. The diabolical mocking of the Green Knight balances the unmalicious quipping of the lord of the northern castle. Even in his most domestic moments Sir Bertilak is sounding the ground bass to the Green Knight theme. Uproarious, self-delighting and unreflecting, the double figure makes an impact like a force of Nature. His humour, his love of the hunt and the chivalric life, make added sense when the mask at last falls, and the Green Knight, the terrible enchanter, compliments the Christian on his virtue. Now almost wistfully in his mind's eye he sees the hero thronging in company 'with paragons of princes', and sadly accepts Gawain's refusal to return to his castle. But we are reminded of the monipresence of evil by the uncanny dismissal of the Green Knight from the story to an undefined but wide realm of activity – 'wherever he would elsewhere'.

It is this ability of the Faerie to span the chasm between Heaven and Hell that makes some of the Romance enchanters more interesting than regular devils with mottoes like 'Evil, be thou my good' (Milton's Satan). These may behave with a daemonic singleness of purpose which bludgeons the reader into terror, but the enchanters, being shape-shifters and servants to both Ormuzd and Ahriman, keep their mystery. The Lady, as I argue on pages 119–21 and 151–3, is a stock enchantress of the school of Morgan the Fay, though she transcends her models in the hands of our poet; but she is so confoundingly attractive that at one moment – and it is the only moment in the whole poem – the poet has almost to give the show away by reminding us that she has 'some other motive besides' love in wishing to seduce the hero. Nevertheless, the reader believes in her sincerity when, bidding Sir Gawain farewell, she commends him to Christ 'with cries of chill sadness', although Gawain would certainly have lost his head had she prevailed.

There is a risk that the modern reader, fancying himself emancipated from mere superstition, will focus excessively and indulgently on that bizarre and wonderful creature, the Green Knight. He may undervalue the virtuous, modest and recognizably human being who initially offers his life to save his uncle's, and remains for almost the whole poem sure that he is going to lose his head to an abominable churlish enchanter. So it is worth emphasizing that the main reason for the existence of the Green Knight and all his works and associates is that the hero may be tested, and that he may reveal his true self in his behaviour while under the threat of death. Gawain must therefore have the last and most important place in these remarks before the reader tackles the poem.

Whatever the circumstances, and whoever he deals with, Gawain is always *courteous*, a term of complex meaning which includes most of the virtues recognized by medieval aristocratic Christian society as we see it in the poem. The courteous man is noble, religious, decent, graceful, eloquent, compassionate, humble, grave; he is capable of both love and chastity, frank in attitude but reserved in behaviour and aware of all the delicacies of personal relationship and public demeanour which go to make up the civilized life. Above all, as D. S. Brewer remarks (Bibliography 5, p. 61), 'it is "courteous" for inner values to correspond to outer. In courtesy external cleanliness signifies inner purity, good manners are a sign of moral goodness, appearance *is* reality.' That is well said. So there is always perfect harmony when the poet moves from external narration of Gawain's actions or words into annotation of his thought processes.

Gawain is an undivided man, whom his creator prevents from being a stereotype of virtue, by warmth of identification, by facing him with trials in which only highly individual qualities will serve him, and by allowing him to express ordinary doubts and fears and to commit a number of peccadilloes. Gawain does not judge others, and even when he imagines his death to be imminent, as when he is talking to the guide who brings him to the Green Chapel, he attributes to them only good motives. This is a hero who applies moral lessons to himself, not others, and then only in the urgency of trying to decide what to do in his successive predicaments. The reader never feels that his fine conduct is inevitable, never regards him as a prig. When a poet can create a profoundly virtuous character, like Gawain, who is not a bore, we must not be surprised when he compounds his achievement at the finale by making the court, on Gawain's return from his ordeals, take the green girdle as a mark of honour, though Gawain regards it as the symbol of his culpable loss of knightly good faith.

Sir Gawain and the Green Knight*

FIT I

I

THE siege and the assault being ceased at Troy,*
The battlements broken down and burnt to brands and ashes,
The treacherous trickster whose treasons there flourished*
Was famed for his falsehood, the foulest on earth.
Aeneas the noble and his knightly kin
Then conquered kingdoms, and kept in their hand
Wellnigh all the wealth of the western lands.
Royal Romulus to Rome first turned,
Set up the city in splendid pomp,
Then named her with his own name, which now she still has:
Ticius founded Tuscany, townships raising,
Longbeard in Lombardy lifted up homes,
And far over the French flood Felix Brutus*
On many spacious slopes set Britain with joy
    And grace;
  Where war and feud and wonder
  Have ruled the realm a space,
  And after, bliss and blunder
  By turns have run their race.

setting — Camelot, feast celebrating Xmas time (new years)

2

AND when this Britain was built by this brave noble,
Here bold men bred, in battle exulting,

*An asterisk indicates that a note referring to the line(s), or to a particular
word or phrase in that line, will be found at the end of the book.

Stirrers of trouble in turbulent times.
Here many a marvel, more than in other lands,
Has befallen by fortune since that far time.
But of all who abode here of Britain's kings,
Arthur was highest in honour, as I have heard;
So I intend to tell you of a true wonder, → intentions.
Which many folk mention as a manifest marvel,
A happening eminent among Arthur's adventures.
Listen to my lay but a little while:*
Straightway shall I speak it, in city as I heard it,
　　　　With tongue;
　　　As scribes have set it duly
　　　In the lore of the land so long,
　　　With letters linking truly
　　　In story bold and strong.

3 — Arthur decanpter +5

THIS king lay at Camelot one Christmastide*
With many mighty lords, manly liegemen,
Members rightly reckoned of the Round Table,
In splendid celebration, seemly and carefree.*   setting-
There tussling in tournament time and again   happy,
Jousted in jollity these gentle knights,   cheery,
Then in court carnival sang catches and danced;   joyful,
For fifteen days the feasting there was full in like measure
With all the meat and merry-making men could devise,
Gladly ringing glee, glorious to hear,
A noble din by day, dancing at night!*
All was happiness in the height in halls and chambers
For lords and their ladies, delectable joy.

With all delights on earth they housed there together,
Saving Christ's self, the most celebrated knights,
The loveliest ladies to live in all time,
And the comeliest king ever to keep court.
For this fine fellowship was in its fair prime★
        Far famed,
    Stood well in heaven's will,
    Its high-souled king acclaimed:
    So hardy a host on hill
    Could not with ease be named.

4

THE year being so young that yester-even saw its birth,★
That day double on the dais were the diners served.
Mass sung and service ended, straight from the chapel
The King and his company came into hall.
Called on with cries from clergy and laity,
Noël was newly announced, named time and again.
Then lords and ladies leaped forth, largesse distributing,★
Offered New Year gifts in high voices, handed them out,
Bustling and bantering about these offerings.
Ladies laughed full loudly, though losing their wealth,
And he that won was not woeful, you may well believe.
All this merriment they made until meal time.
Then in progress to their places they passed after washing,
In authorized order, the high-ranking first;★
With glorious Guinevere, gay in the midst,
On the princely platform with its precious hangings
Of splendid silk at the sides, a state over her

Of rich tapestry of Toulouse and Turkestan
Brilliantly embroidered with the best gems
Of warranted worth that wealth at any time
      Could buy.
   Fairest of form was this queen,
   Glinting and grey of eye;*
   No man could say he had seen
   A lovelier, but with a lie.

5

BUT Arthur would not eat until all were served.
He was charming and cheerful, child-like and gay,
And loving active life, little did he favour
Lying down for long or lolling on a seat,
So robust his young blood and his beating brain.
Still, he was stirred now by something else:
His noble announcement that he never would eat*
On such a fair feast-day till informed in full
Of some unusual adventure, as yet untold,
Of some momentous marvel that he might believe,
About ancestors, or arms, or other high theme;
Or till a stranger should seek out a strong knight of his,
To join with him in jousting, in jeopardy to lay
Life against life, each allowing the other
The favour of Fortune, the fairer lot.
Such was the King's custom when he kept court,
At every fine feast among his free retinue
      In hall.
   So he throve amid the throng,
   A ruler royal and tall,

24

TRUTH!

Still standing staunch and strong,
And young like the year withal.

6

Wants to win our trust

narrator's intent-true wonder, not exaggerated

ERECT stood the strong King, stately of mien,
Trifling time with talk before the topmost table.
Good Gawain was placed at Guinevere's side,
And Agravain of the Hard Hand sat on the other side,*
Both the King's sister's sons, staunchest of knights.
Above, Bishop Baldwin began the board,*
And Ywain, Urien's son ate next to him.
These were disposed on the dais and with dignity served,
And many mighty men next, marshalled at side tables.
Then the first course came in with such cracking of trumpets,
(Whence bright bedecked blazons in banners hung)
Such din of drumming and a deal of fine piping,*
Such wild warbles whelming and echoing
That hearts were uplifted high at the strains.
Then delicacies and dainties were delivered to the guests,
Fresh food in foison, such freight of full dishes
That space was scarce at the social tables
For the several soups set before them in silver
      On the cloth.
   Each feaster made free with the fare,
   Took lightly and nothing loth;
   Twelve plates were for every pair,*
   Good beer and bright wine both.

setting the scene

wealth, cheery, celebrate

jousting (sporting)

active, generous

so much food, luxury. extravagent fiest

written in alliterative verse.

Narrator- trying to find voice

"letters linking truly"

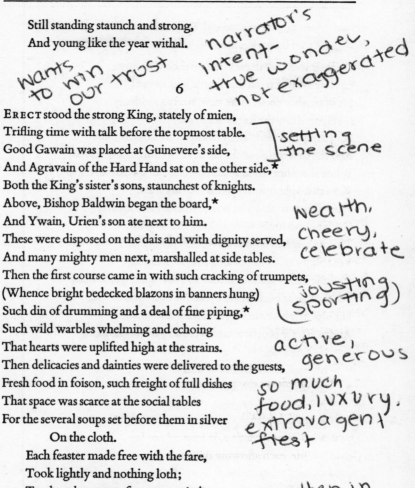

7

Of their meal I shall mention no more just now,
For it is evident to all that ample was served;
Now another noise, quite new, neared suddenly,
Likely to allow the liege lord to eat;*
For barely had the blast of trump abated one minute
And the first course in the court been courteously served,
When there heaved in at the hall door an awesome fellow
Who in height outstripped all earthly men.
From throat to thigh he was so thickset and square,
His loins and limbs were so long and so great,
That he was half a giant on earth, I believe;
Yet mainly and most of all a man he seemed,
And the handsomest of horsemen, though huge, at that;
For though at back and at breast his body was broad,
His hips and haunches were elegant and small,
And perfectly proportioned were all parts of the man,
     As seen.
   Men gaped at the hue of him
   Ingrained in garb and mien,
   A fellow fiercely grim,
   And all a glittering green.

8

And garments of green girt the fellow about –
A two-third length tunic, tight at the waist,
A comely cloak on top, accomplished with lining
Of the finest fur to be found, made of one piece,

26

Marvellous fur-trimmed material, with matching hood
Lying back from his locks and laid on his shoulders;
Fitly held-up hose, in hue the same green,
That was caught at the calf, with clinking spurs beneath
Of bright gold on bases of embroidered silk,
But no iron shoe armoured that horseman's feet.*
And verily his vesture was all vivid green,
So were the bars on his belt and the brilliants set
In ravishing array on the rich accoutrements
About himself and his saddle on silken work.
It would be tedious to tell a tithe of the trifles
Embossed and embroidered, such as birds and flies,
In gay green gauds, with gold everywhere.*
The breast-hangings of the horse, its haughty crupper,
The enamelled knobs and nails on its bridle,
And the stirrups that he stood on, were all stained with the same;
So were the splendid saddle-skirts and bows
That ever glimmered and glinted with their green stones.
The steed that he spurred on was similar in hue

      To the sight,
   Green and huge of grain,
   Mettlesome in might
   And brusque with bit and rein –
   A steed to serve that knight!

9

YES, garbed all in green was the gallant rider,
And the hair of his head was the same hue as his horse,
And floated finely like a fan round his shoulders;

27

And a great bushy beard on his breast flowing down,
With the heavy hair hanging from his head,
Was shorn below the shoulder, sheared right round,
So that half his arms were under the encircling hair,
Covered as by a king's cape, that closes at the neck.
The mane of that mighty horse, much like the beard,
Well crisped and combed, was copiously plaited
With twists of twining gold, twinkling in the green,
First a green gossamer, a golden one next.
His flowing tail and forelock followed suit,
And both were bound with bands of bright green,
Ornamented to the end with exquisite stones,
While a thong running through them threaded on high
Many bright golden bells, burnished and ringing.
Such a horse, such a horseman, in the whole wide world
Was never seen or observed by those assembled before,
        Not one.
    Lightning-like he seemed
    And swift to strike and stun.
    His dreadful blows, men deemed,
    Once dealt, meant death was done.

10

YET hauberk and helmet had he none,
Nor plastron nor plate-armour proper to combat,
Nor shield for shoving, nor sharp spear for lunging;
But he held a holly cluster in one hand, holly*
That is greenest when groves are gaunt and bare,
And an axe in his other hand, huge and monstrous,

28

A hideous helmet-smasher for anyone to tell of;★
The head of that axe was an ell-rod long.
Of green hammered gold and steel was the socket,
And the blade was burnished bright, with a broad edge,
Acutely honed for cutting, as keenest razors are.
The grim man gripped it by its great strong handle,
Which was wound with iron all the way to the end,
And graven in green with graceful designs.
A cord curved round it, was caught at the head,
Then hitched to the haft at intervals in loops,
With costly tassels attached thereto in plenty
On bosses of bright green embroidered richly.
In he rode, and up the hall, this man,
Driving towards the high dais, dreading no danger.
He gave no one a greeting, but glared over all.
His opening utterance was, 'Who and where
Is the governor of this gathering? Gladly would I
Behold him with my eyes and have speech with him.'

> He frowned;
>> Took note of every knight
>> As he ramped and rode around;
>> Then stopped to study who might
>> Be the noble most renowned.

II

THE assembled folk stared, long scanning the fellow,
For all men marvelled what it might mean
That a horseman and his horse should have such a colour
As to grow green as grass, and greener yet, it seemed,

29

More gaudily glowing than green enamel on gold.
Those standing studied him and sidled towards him★
With all the world's wonder as to what he would do.
For astonishing sights they had seen, but such a one never;
Therefore a phantom from Fairyland the folk there deemed him.
So even the doughty were daunted and dared not reply,★
All sitting stock-still, astounded by his voice.
Throughout the high hall was a hush like death;
Suddenly as if all had slipped into sleep, their voices were

> At rest;
> Hushed not wholly for fear,
> But some at honour's behest;
> But let him whom all revere
> Greet that gruesome guest.

12

FOR Arthur sensed an exploit before the high dais,
And accorded him courteous greeting, no craven he,
Saying to him, 'Sir knight, you are certainly welcome.
I am head of this house: Arthur is my name.
Please deign to dismount and dwell with us
Till you impart your purpose, at a proper time.'
'May he that sits in heaven help me,' said the knight,★
'But my intention was not to tarry in this turreted hall.
But as your reputation, royal sir, is raised up so high,
And your castle and cavaliers are accounted the best,
The mightiest of mail-clad men in mounted fighting,
The most warlike, the worthiest the world has bred,
Most valiant to vie with in virile contests,
And as chivalry is shown here, so I am assured,

At this time, I tell you, that has attracted me here.
By this branch that I bear, you may be certain
That I proceed in peace, no peril seeking;
For had I fared forth in fighting gear,
My hauberk and helmet, both at home now,
My shield and sharp spear, all shining bright,
And other weapons to wield, I would have brought;
However, as I wish for no war here, I wear soft clothes.
But if you are as bold as brave men affirm,
You will gladly grant me the good sport I demand
    By right.'
  Then Arthur answer gave:
  'If you, most noble knight,
  Unarmoured combat crave,
  We'll fail you not in fight.'

13

'No, it is not combat I crave, for come to that,
On this bench only beardless boys are sitting.
If I were hasped in armour on a high steed,
No man among you could match me, your might being meagre.
So I crave in this court a Christmas game,
For it is Yuletide and New Year, and young men abound here.
If any in this household is so hardy in spirit,
Of such mettlesome mind and so madly rash
As to strike a strong blow in return for another,
I shall offer to him this fine axe freely;
This axe, which is heavy enough, to handle as he please.
And I shall bide the first blow, as bare as I sit here.
If some intrepid man is tempted to try what I suggest,

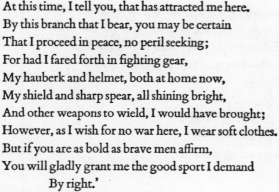

31

Let him leap towards me and lay hold of this weapon,
Acquiring clear possession of it, no claim from me ensuing.
Then shall I stand up to his stroke, quite still on this floor –
So long as I shall have leave to launch a return blow
          Unchecked.
      Yet he shall have a year
      And a day's reprieve, I direct.
      Now hasten and let me hear
      Who answers, to what effect.'

14

IF he had astonished them at the start, yet stiller now
Were the henchmen in hall, both high and low.
The rider wrenched himself round in his saddle
And rolled his red eyes about roughly and strangely,*
Bending his brows, bristling and bright, on all,
His beard swaying as he strained to see who would rise.
When none came to accord with him, he coughed aloud,
Then pulled himself up proudly, and spoke as follows:
'What, is this Arthur's house, the honour of which
Is bruited abroad so abundantly?
Has your pride disappeared? Your prowess gone?
Your victories, your valour, your vaunts, where are they?
The revel and renown of the Round Table
Is now overwhelmed by a word from one man's voice,
For all flinch for fear from a fight not begun!'
Upon this, he laughed so loudly that the lord grieved.
His fair features filled with blood
          For shame.
      He raged as roaring gale;

His followers felt the same.
The King, not one to quail,
To that cavalier then came.

15

'BY heaven,' then said Arthur, 'What you ask is foolish,
But as you firmly seek folly, find it you shall.
No good man here is aghast at your great words.
Hand me your axe now, for heaven's sake,
And I shall bestow the boon you bid us give.'
He sprang towards him swiftly, seized it from his hand,
And fiercely the other fellow footed the floor.
Now Arthur had his axe, and holding it by the haft
Swung it about sternly, as if to strike with it.
The strong man stood before him, stretched to his full height,
Higher than any in the hall by a head and more.
Stern of face he stood there, stroking his beard,
Turning down his tunic in a tranquil manner,
Less unmanned and dismayed by the mighty strokes★
Than if a banqueter at the bench had brought him a drink
          Of wine.
     Then Gawain at Guinevere's side★
     Bowed and spoke his design:
     'Before all, King, confide
     This fight to me. May it be mine.'

16

'IF you would, worthy lord,' said Gawain to the King,
'Bid me stir from this seat and stand beside you,

Allowing me without lese-majesty to leave the table,
And if my liege lady were not displeased thereby,
I should come there to counsel you before this court of nobles.
For it appears unmeet to me, as manners go,
When your hall hears uttered such a haughty request,
Though you gladly agree, for you to grant it yourself,
When on the benches about you many such bold men sit,
Under heaven, I hold, the highest-mettled,
There being no braver knights when battle is joined.
I am the weakest, the most wanting in wisdom, I know,
And my life, if lost, would be least missed, truly.
Only through your being my uncle, am I to be valued;
No bounty but your blood in my body do I know.
And since this affair is too foolish to fall to you,
And I first asked it of you, make it over to me;
And if I fail to speak fittingly, let this full court judge
          Without blame.'
          Then wisely they whispered of it,
          And after, all said the same:
          That the crowned King should be quit,
          And Gawain given the game.

17

THEN the King commanded the courtly knight to rise.
He directly uprose, approached courteously,
Knelt low to his liege lord, laid hold of the weapon;
And he graciously let him have it, lifted up his hand
And gave him God's blessing, gladly urging him
To be strong in spirit and stout of sinew.
'Cousin, take care,' said the King, 'To chop once,

34

And if you strike with success, certainly I think
You will take the return blow without trouble in time.'
Gripping the great axe, Gawain goes to the man
Who awaits him unwavering, not quailing at all.
Then said to Sir Gawain the stout knight in green,
'Let us affirm our pact freshly, before going farther.
I beg you, bold sir, to be so good
As to tell me your true name, as I trust you to.'
'In good faith,' said the good knight, 'Gawain is my name,
And whatever happens after, I offer you this blow,
And in twelve months' time I shall take the return blow
With whatever weapon you wish, and with no one else
          Shall I strive.'
     The other with pledge replied,
     'I'm the merriest man alive
     It's a blow from you I must bide,
     Sir Gawain, so may I thrive.'

18

'By God,' said the Green Knight, 'Sir Gawain, I rejoice
That I shall have from your hand what I have asked for here.
And you have gladly gone over, in good discourse,
The covenant I requested of the King in full,
Except that you shall assent, swearing in truth,
To seek me yourself, in such place as you think
To find me under the firmament, and fetch your payment
For what you deal me today before this dignified gathering.'
'How shall I hunt for you? How find your home?'
Said Gawain, 'By God that made me, I go in ignorance;
Nor, knight, do I know your name or your court.

35

But instruct me truly thereof, and tell me your name,
And I shall wear out my wits to find my way there;
Here is my oath on it, in absolute honour!'
'That is enough this New Year, no more is needed,'
Said the gallant in green to Gawain the courteous,
'To tell you the truth, when I have taken the blow
After you have duly dealt it, I shall directly inform you
About my house and my home and my own name.
Then you may keep your covenant, and call on me,
And if I waft you no words, then well may you prosper,
Stay long in your own land and look for no further
      Trial.
        Now grip your weapon grim;
        Let us see your fighting style.'
        'Gladly,' said Gawain to him,
        Stroking the steel the while.

19

ON the ground the Green Knight graciously stood,
With head slightly slanting to expose the flesh.
His long and lovely locks he laid over his crown,
Baring the naked neck for the business now due.
Gawain gripped his axe and gathered it on high,
Advanced the left foot before him on the ground,
And slashed swiftly down on the exposed part,
So that the sharp blade sheared through, shattering the bones,
Sank deep in the sleek flesh, split it in two,
And the scintillating steel struck the ground.
The fair head fell from the neck, struck the floor,

And people spurned it as it rolled around.*
Blood spurted from the body, bright against the green.
Yet the fellow did not fall, nor falter one whit,
But stoutly sprang forward on legs still sturdy,
Roughly reached out among the ranks of nobles,
Seized his splendid head and straightway lifted it.
Then he strode to his steed, snatched the bridle,
Stepped into the stirrup and swung aloft,
Holding his head in his hand by the hair.
He settled himself in the saddle as steadily
As if nothing had happened to him, though he had
        No head.
    He twisted his trunk about,
    That gruesome body that bled;
    He caused much dread and doubt
    By the time his say was said.

20

FOR he held the head in his hand upright,
Pointed the face at the fairest in fame on the dais;*
And it lifted its eyelids and looked glaringly,
And menacingly said with its mouth as you may now hear:
'Be prepared to perform what you promised, Gawain;
Seek faithfully till you find me, my fine fellow,
According to your oath in this hall in these knights' hearing.
Go to the Green Chapel without gainsaying to get
Such a stroke as you have struck. Strictly you deserve
That due redemption on the day of New Year.
As the Knight of the Green Chapel I am known to many;

Therefore if you ask for me, I shall be found.
So come, or else be called coward accordingly!'
Then he savagely swerved, sawing at the reins,
Rushed out at the hall door, his head in his hand,
And the flint-struck fire flew up from the hooves.
What place he departed to no person there knew, ★
Nor could any account be given of the country he had come from.
       What then?★
  At the Green Knight Gawain and King
  Grinned and laughed again;
  But plainly approved the thing
  As a marvel in the world of men.

21

THOUGH honoured King Arthur was at heart astounded,
He let no sign of it be seen, but said clearly
To the comely queen in courtly speech,
'Do not be dismayed, dear lady, today:
Such cleverness comes well at Christmastide,
Like the playing of interludes, laughter and song,
As lords and ladies delight in courtly carols.
However, I am now able to eat the repast,
Having seen, I must say, a sight to wonder at.'
He glanced at Sir Gawain, and gracefully said,
'Now sir, hang up your axe: you have hewn enough.'★
And on the backcloth above the dais it was boldly hung
Where all men might mark it and marvel at it
And with truthful testimony tell the wonder of it.
Then to the table the two went together,
The King and the constant knight, and keen men served them

Double portions of each dainty with all due dignity,
All manner of meat, and minstrelsy too.
Daylong they delighted till darkness came
        To their shores.
        Now Gawain give a thought,
        Lest peril make you pause
        In seeking out the sport
        That you have claimed as yours.

— What are Sir Gawain's
  outstanding characteristics?

— What do the actions +
  reactions of Arthur +
  the members of his court
  suggest about the values
  of Medieval society?

FIT II

22

SUCH earnest of noble action had Arthur at New Year,
For he was avid to hear exploits vaunted.
Though starved of such speeches when seated at first,
Now had they high matter indeed, their hands full of it.
Gawain was glad to begin the games in hall,
But though the end be heavy, have no wonder,
For if men are spritely in spirit after strong drink,
Soon the year slides past, never the same twice;
There is no foretelling its fulfilment from the start.
Yes, this Yuletide passed and the year following;*
Season after season in succession went by.
After Christmas comes the crabbed Lenten time,
Which forces on the flesh fish and food yet plainer.
Then weather more vernal wars with the wintry world,
The cold ebbs and declines, the clouds lift,
In shining showers the rain sheds warmth
And falls upon the fair plain, where flowers appear;
The grassy lawns and groves alike are garbed in green;
Birds prepare to build, and brightly sing
The solace of the ensuing summer that soothes hill
     And dell.
    By hedgerows rank and rich
    The blossoms bloom and swell,
    And sounds of sweetest pitch
    From lovely woodlands well.

23

THEN comes the season of summer with soft winds,
When Zephyrus himself breathes on seeds and herbs.
In paradise is the plant that springs in the open
When the dripping dew drops from its leaves,
And it bears the blissful gleam of the bright sun.
Then Harvest comes hurrying, urging it on,
Warning it because of winter to wax ripe soon;
He drives the dust to rise with the drought he brings,
Forcing it to fly up from the face of the earth.
Wrathful winds in raging skies wrestle with the sun;
Leaves are lashed loose from the trees and lie on the ground
And the grass becomes grey which was green before.
What rose from root at first now ripens and rots;
So the year in passing yields its many yesterdays,
And winter returns, as the way of the world is,
      I swear;
   So came the Michaelmas moon,
   With winter threatening there,
   And Gawain considered soon
   The fell way he must fare.

24

YET he stayed in hall with Arthur till All Saints' Day,*
When Arthur provided plentifully, especially for Gawain,
A rich feast and high revelry at the Round Table.
The gallant lords and gay ladies grieved for Gawain,
Anxious on his account; but all the same

They mentioned only matters of mirthful import,
Joylessly joking for that gentle knight's sake.
For after dinner with drooping heart he addressed his uncle
And spoke plainly of his departure, putting it thus:
'Now, liege lord of my life, I beg my leave of you.
You know the kind of covenant it is: I care little
To tell over the trials of it, trifling as they are,
But I am bound to bear the blow and must be gone tomorrow
To seek the gallant in green, as God sees fit to guide me.'
Then the most courtly in that company came together,
Ywain and Eric and others in troops,★
Sir Dodinal the Fierce, The Duke of Clarence,★
Lancelot and Lionel and Lucan the Good,★
Sir Bors and Sir Bedivere, both strong men,★
And many admired knights, with Mador of the Gate.★
All the company of the court came near to the King
With carking care in their hearts, to counsel the knight.
Much searing sorrow was suffered in the hall
That such a gallant man as Gawain should go in quest
To suffer a savage blow, and his sword no more
          Should bear.
      Said Gawain, gay of cheer,
      'Whether fate be foul or fair,
      Why falter I or fear?
      What should man do but dare?'

                    25

HE dwelt there all that day, and at dawn on the morrow
Asked for his armour. Every item was brought.

First a crimson carpet was cast over the floor
And the great pile of gilded war-gear glittered upon it.
The strong man stepped on it, took the steel in hand.
The doublet he dressed in was dear Turkestan stuff;
Then came the courtly cape, cut with skill,
Finely lined with fur, and fastened close.
Then they set the steel shoes on the strong man's feet,
Lapped his legs in steel with lovely greaves,
Complete with knee-pieces, polished bright
And connecting at the knee with gold-knobbed hinges.
Then came the cuisses, which cunningly enclosed
His thighs thick of thew, and which thongs secured.
Next the hauberk, interlinked with argent steel rings
Which rested on rich material, wrapped the warrior round.
He had polished armour on arms and elbows,
Glinting and gay, and gloves of metal,
And all the goodly gear to give help whatever
    Betide;
      With surcoat richly wrought,
      Gold spurs attached in pride,
      A silken sword-belt athwart,
      And steadfast blade at his side.

26

WHEN he was hasped in armour his harness was noble;
The least lace or loop was lustrous with gold.
So, harnessed as he was, he heard his mass
As it was offered at the high altar in worship.
Then he came to the King and his court-fellows,

Took leave with loving courtesy of lord and lady,
Who commended him to Christ and kissed him farewell.
By now Gringolet had been got ready, and girt with a saddle★
That gleamed most gaily with many golden fringes,
Everywhere nailed newly for this noble occasion.
The bridle was embossed and bound with bright gold;
So were the furnishings of the fore-harness and the fine skirts.
The crupper and the caparison accorded with the saddle-bows,
And all was arrayed on red with nails of richest gold,
Which glittered and glanced like gleams of the sun.
Then his casque, equipped with clasps of great strength
And padded inside, he seized and swiftly kissed;
It towered high on his head and was hasped at the back,
With a brilliant silk band over the burnished neck-guard,
Embroidered and bossed with the best gems
On broad silken borders, with birds about the seams,
Such as parrots painted with periwinkles between,★
And turtles and true-love-knots traced as thickly
As if many beauties in a bower had been busy seven winters
   Thereabout.
  The circlet on his head
  Was prized more precious no doubt,
  And perfectly diamonded,
  Threw a gleaming lustre out.

27

THEN they showed him the shield of shining gules,★
With the Pentangle in pure gold depicted thereon.★
He brandished it by the baldric, and about his neck
He slung it in a seemly way, and it suited him well.

44

And I intend to tell you, though I tarry therefore,
Why the Pentangle is proper to this prince of knights.
It is a symbol which Solomon conceived once
To betoken holy truth, by its intrinsic right,
For it is a figure which has five points,
And each line overlaps and is locked with another;
And it is endless everywhere, and the English call it,
In all the land, I hear, the Endless Knot.
Therefore it goes with Sir Gawain and his gleaming armour,
For, ever faithful in five things, each in fivefold manner,
Gawain was reputed good and, like gold well refined,
He was devoid of all villainy, every virtue displaying
          In the field.
          Thus this Pentangle new
          He carried on coat and shield,
          As a man of troth most true
          And knightly name annealed.

28

FIRST he was found faultless in his five wits.★
Next, his five fingers never failed the knight,
And all his trust on earth was in the five wounds
Which came to Christ on the Cross, as the Creed tells.
And whenever the bold man was busy on the battlefield,
Through all other things he thought on this,
That his prowess all depended on the five pure Joys★
That the holy Queen of Heaven had of her Child.
Accordingly the courteous knight had that queen's image
Etched on the inside of his armoured shield,
So that when he beheld her, his heart did not fail.

45

The fifth five I find the famous man practised
Were – Liberality and Lovingkindness leading the rest;*
Then his Continence and Courtesy, which were never corrupted;
And Piety, the surpassing virtue. These pure five
Were more firmly fixed on that fine man
Than on any other, and every multiple,
Each interlocking with another, had no end,
Being fixed to five points which never failed,
Never assembling on one side, nor sundering either,
With no end at any angle; nor can I find
Where the design started or proceeded to its end.
Thus on his shining shield this knot was shaped
Royally in red gold upon red gules.
That is the pure Pentangle, so people who are wise
     Are taught.
    Now Gawain was ready and gay;
    His spear he promptly caught
    And gave them all good day
    For ever, as he thought.

29

HE struck the steed with his spurs and sprang on his way
So forcefully that the fire flew up from the flinty stones.
All who saw that seemly sight were sick at heart,
And all said to each other softly, in the same breath,
In care for that comely knight, 'By Christ, it is evil
That yon lord should be lost, who lives so nobly!*
To find his fellow on earth in faith is not easy.
It would have been wiser to have worked more warily,

And to have dubbed the dear man a duke of the realm.

hero

A magnificent master of men he might have been,
And so had a happier fate than to be utterly destroyed,
Beheaded by an unearthly being out of arrogance.
Who supposed the Prince would approve such counsel
As is giddily given in Christmas games by knights?'
Many were the watery tears that whelmed from weeping eyes,
When on quest that worthy knight went from the court
> That day.
>> He faltered not nor feared,
>> But quickly went his way;
>> His road was rough and weird,
>> Or so the stories say.

30

N o w the gallant Sir Gawain in God's name goes
Riding through the realm of Britain, no rapture in his mind.
Often the long night he lay alone and companionless,
And did not find in front of him food of his choice;
He had no comrade but his courser in the country woods and hills,
No traveller to talk to on the track but God,
Till he was nearly nigh to Northern Wales.*
The isles of Anglesey he kept always on his left,
And fared across the fords by the foreshore
Over at Holy Head to the other side
Into the wilderness of Wirral, where few dwelled
To whom God or good-hearted man gave his love.
And always as he went, he asked whomever he met
If they knew or had knowledge of a knight in green,

looking for green knight deer?

heroic

quality of fighting

Or could guide him to the ground where a green chapel stood.
And there was none but said him nay, for never in their lives
Had they set eyes on someone of such a hue
        As green.
    His way was wild and strange
    By dreary hill and dean.
    His mood would many times change
    Before that fane was seen.

31

good quote about amount of fighting

HE rode far from his friends, a forsaken man,
Scaling many cliffs in country unknown.
At every bank or beach where the brave man crossed water,*
He found a foe in front of him, except by a freak of chance,
And so foul and fierce a one that he was forced to fight.
So many marvels did the man meet in the mountains,
It would be too tedious to tell a tenth of them.
He had death-struggles with dragons, did battle with wolves,
Warred with wild men who dwelt among the crags,*
Battled with bulls and bears and boars at other times,
And ogres that panted after him on the high fells.
Had he not been doughty in endurance and dutiful to God,
Doubtless he would have been done to death time and again.
Yet the warring little worried him; worse was the winter,
When the cold clear water cascaded from the clouds
And froze before it could fall to the fallow earth.
Half-slain by the sleet, he slept in his armour
Night after night among the naked rocks,
Where the cold streams splashed from the steep crests
Or hung high over his head in hard icicles.

48

So in peril and pain, in parlous plight, *aaaa*
This knight covered the country till Christmas Eve
   Alone;
  And he that eventide
  To Mary made his moan,
  And begged her be his guide
  Till some shelter should be shown.

32

MERRILY in the morning by a mountain he rode
Into a wondrously wild wooded cleft,
With high hills on each side overpeering a forest
Of huge hoary oaks, a hundred together.
The hazel and the hawthorn were intertwined
With rough ragged moss trailing everywhere,
And on the bleak branches birds in misery
Piteously piped away, pinched with cold.
The gallant knight on Gringolet galloped under them
Through many a swamp and marsh, a man all alone,
Fearing lest he should fail, through adverse fortune,
To see the service of him who that same night
Was born of a bright maiden to banish our strife.
And so sighing he said, 'I beseech thee Lord,
And thee Mary, mildest mother so dear,
That in some haven with due honour I may hear Mass
And Matins tomorrow morning: meekly I ask it,
And promptly thereto I pray my Pater and Ave
   And Creed.'
  He crossed himself and cried
  For his sins, and said, 'Christ speed

My cause, his cross my guide!'
So prayed he, spurring his steed.

33

THRICE the sign of the Saviour on himself he had made,★
When in the wood he was aware of a dwelling with a moat
On a promontory above a plateau, penned in by the boughs
And tremendous trunks of trees, and trenched about;
The comeliest castle that ever a knight owned,
It was pitched on a plain, with a park all round,
Impregnably palisaded with pointed stakes,
And containing many trees in its two-mile circumference.
The courteous knight contemplated the castle from one side
As it shimmered and shone through the shining oaks.
Then humbly he took off his helmet and offered thanks
To Jesus and Saint Julian, gentle patrons both,★
Who had given him grace and gratified his wish.
'Now grant it be good lodging!' the gallant knight said.
Then he goaded Gringolet with his golden heels,
And mostly by chance emerged on the main highway,
Which brought the brave man to the bridge's end
          With one cast.
     The drawbridge vertical,
     The gates shut firm and fast,
     The well-provided wall –
     It blenched at never a blast.

34

THE knight, still on his steed, stayed on the bank

great description

Of the deep double ditch that drove round the place.*
The wall went into the water wonderfully deep,
And then to a huge height upwards it reared
In hard hewn stone, up to the cornice;
Built under the battlements in the best style, courses jutted
And turrets protruded between, constructed
With loopholes in plenty with locking shutters.
No better barbican had ever been beheld by that knight.
And inside he could see a splendid high hall
With towers and turrets on top, all tipped with crenellations,
And pretty pinnacles placed along its length,
With carved copes, cunningly worked.
Many chalk-white chimneys the chevalier saw
On the tops of towers twinkling whitely,
So many painted pinnacles sprinkled everywhere,
Congregated in clusters among the crenellations,
That it appeared like a prospect of paper patterning.*
To the gallant knight on Gringolet it seemed good enough
If he could ever gain entrance to the inner court,
And harbour in that house while Holy Day lasted,
          Well cheered.
     He hailed, and at a height
     A civil porter appeared,
     Who welcomed the wandering knight,
     And his inquiry heard.

35

'Good sir,' said Gawain, 'Will you give my message
To the high lord of this house, that I ask for lodging?'
'Yes, by Saint Peter,' replied the porter, 'and I think★
You may lodge here as long as you like, sir knight.'
Then away he went eagerly, and swiftly returned
With a host of well-wishers to welcome the knight.
They let down the drawbridge and in a dignified way
Came out and did honour to him, kneeling
Courteously on the cold ground to accord him worthy welcome.
They prayed him to pass the portcullis, now pulled up high,
And he readily bid them rise and rode over the bridge.
Servants held his saddle while he stepped down,
And his steed was stabled by sturdy men in plenty.
Strong knights and squires descended then
To bring the bold warrior blithely into hall.
When he took off his helmet, many hurried forward
To receive it and to serve this stately man,
And his bright sword and buckler were both taken as well.
Then graciously he greeted each gallant knight,
And many proud men pressed forward to pay their respects.
Garbed in his fine garments, he was guided to the hall,
Where a fine fire was burning fiercely on the hearth.
Then the prince of those people appeared from his chamber
To meet in mannerly style the man in his hall.
'You are welcome to dwell here as you wish,' he said,
'Treat everything as your own, and have what you please
          In this place.'
     'I yield my best thanks yet:
     May Christ make good your grace!'

Said Gawain and, gladly met,
They clasped in close embrace.

36

GAWAIN gazed at the gallant who had greeted him well
And it seemed to him the stronghold possessed a brave lord,*
A powerful man in his prime, of stupendous size.
Broad and bright was his beard, all beaver-hued;
Strong and sturdy he stood on his stalwart legs;
His face was fierce as fire, free was his speech,
And he seemed in good sooth a suitable man
To be prince of a people with companions of mettle.
This prince led him to an apartment and expressly commanded
That a man be commissioned to minister to Gawain;
And at his bidding a band of men bent to serve
Brought him to a beautiful room where the bedding was noble.
The bed-curtains, of brilliant silk with bright gold hems,
Had skilfully-sewn coverlets with comely facings,
And the fairest fur on the fringes was worked.
With ruddy gold rings on the cords ran the curtains;
Toulouse and Turkestan tapestries on the wall
And fine carpets underfoot, on the floor, were fittingly matched.
There amid merry talk the man was disrobed,
And stripped of his battle-sark and his splendid clothes.
Retainers readily brought him rich robes
Of the choicest kind to choose from and change into.
In a trice when he took one, and was attired in it,
And it sat on him in style, with spreading skirts,
It certainly seemed to those assembled as if spring*
In all its hues were evident before them;

His lithe limbs below the garment were gleaming with beauty.
Jesus never made, so men judged, more gentle and handsome
>   A knight:
>   From wherever in the world he were,
>   At sight it seemed he might
>   Be a prince without a peer
>   In field where fell men fight.

37

A T the chimneyed hearth where charcoal burned, a chair was placed
For Sir Gawain in gracious style, gorgeously decked
With cushions on quilted work, both cunningly wrought;
And then on that man a magnificent mantle was thrown,
A gleaming garment gorgeously embroidered,
Fairly lined with fur, the finest skins
Of ermine on earth, and his hood of the same.
In that splendid seat he sat in dignity,
And warmth came to him at once, bringing well-being.
In a trice on fine trestles a table was put up,
Then covered with a cloth shining clean and white,
And set with silver spoons, salt-cellars and overlays.
The worthy knight washed willingly, and went to his meat.
In seemly enough style servants brought him*
Several fine soups, seasoned lavishly
Twice-fold, as is fitting, and fish of all kinds –
Some baked in bread, some browned on coals,
Some seethed, some stewed and savoured with spice,
But always subtly sauced, and so the man liked it.
The gentle knight generously judged it a feast,

54

And often said so, while the servers spurred him on thus
      As he ate:
  'This present penance do;
  It soon shall be offset.'
  The knight rejoiced anew,
  For the wine his spirits whet.

38

THEN in seemly style they searchingly inquired,
Putting to the prince private questions,
So that he courteously conceded he came of that court
Where high-souled Arthur held sway alone,
Ruler most royal of the Round Table;
And that Sir Gawain himself now sat in the house,
Having come that Christmas, by course of fortune.
Loudly laughed the lord when he learned what knight*
He had in his house; such happiness it brought
That all the men within the moat made merry,
And promptly appeared in the presence of Gawain,
To whose person are proper all prowess and worth,
And pure and perfect manners, and praises unceasing.
His reputation rates first in the ranks of men.
Each knight neared his neighbour and softly said,
'Now we shall see displayed the seemliest manners*
And the faultless figures of virtuous discourse.
Without asking we may hear how to hold conversation
Since we have seized upon this scion of good breeding.
God has given us of his grace good measure
In granting us such a guest as Gawain is,

55

When, contented at Christ's birth, the courtiers shall sit
        And sing.
    This noble knight will prove
    What manners the mighty bring;
    His converse of courtly love
    Shall spur our studying.'

39

WHEN the fine man had finished his food and risen,
It was nigh and near to the night's mid-hour.
Priests to their prayers paced their way
And rang the bells royally, as rightly they should,
To honour that high feast with evensong.
The lord inclines to prayer, the lady too;
Into her private pew she prettily walks;
Gawain advances gaily and goes there quickly,
But the lord gripped his gown and guided him to his seat,
Acknowledged him by name and benevolently said
In the whole world he was the most welcome of men.
Gawain spoke his gratitude, they gravely embraced,
And sat in serious mood the whole service through.
Then the lady had a longing to look on the knight;
With her bevy of beauties she abandoned her pew.
Most beautiful of body and bright of complexion,★
Most winsome in ways of all women alive,
She seemed to Sir Gawain, excelling Guinevere.
To squire that splendid dame, he strode through the chancel.
Another lady led her by the left hand,
A matron, much older, past middle age,
Who was highly honoured by an escort of squires.

56

Most unlike to look on those ladies were,
For if the one was winsome, then withered was the other.
Hues rich and rubious were arrayed on the one,
Rough wrinkles on the other rutted the cheeks.
Kerchiefed with clear pearls clustering was the one,
Her breast and bright throat bare to the sight,
Shining like sheen of snow shed on the hills;
The other was swathed with a wimple wound to the throat
And choking her swarthy chin in chalk-white veils.
On her forehead were folded enveloping silks,
Trellised about with trefoils and tiny rings.
Nothing was bare on that beldame but the black brows,
The two eyes, protruding nose and stark lips,
And those were a sorry sight and exceedingly bleary:
A grand lady, God knows, of greatness in the world
            Well tried!
        Her body was stumpy and squat,
        Her buttocks bulging and wide;
        More pleasure a man could plot
        With the sweet one at her side.

40

WHEN Gawain had gazed on that gracious-looking creature
He gained leave of the lord to go along with the ladies.
He saluted the senior, sweeping a low bow,
But briefly embraced the beautiful one,
Kissing her in courtly style and complimenting her.
They craved his acquaintance and he quickly requested
To be their faithful follower, if they would so favour him.
They took him between them, and talking, they led him

57

To a high room. By the hearth they asked first
For spices, which unstintingly men sped to bring,
And always with heart-warming, heady wine.
In lovingkindness the lord leaped up repeatedly
And many times reminded them that mirth should flow;
Elaborately lifted up his hood, looped it on a spear,
And offered it as a mark of honour to whoever should prove able
To make the most mirth that merry Yuletide.
'And I shall essay, I swear, to strive with the best
Before this garment goes from me, by my good friends' help.'
So with his mirth the mighty lord made things merry
To gladden Sir Gawain with games in hall
           That night;
     Until, the time being spent,
     The lord demanded light.★
     Gawain took his leave and went
     To rest in rare delight.

41

O N that morning when men call to mind the birth
Of our dear Lord born to die for our destiny,
Joy waxes in dwellings the world over for his sake:
And so it befell there on the feast day with fine fare.
Both at main meals and minor repasts strong men served
Rare dishes with fine dressings to the dais company.
Highest, in the place of honour, the ancient crone sat,
And the lord, so I believe, politely next.
Together sat Gawain and the gay lady★
In mid-table, where the meal was mannerly served first;
And after throughout the hall, as was held best,

Each gallant by degree was graciously served.
There was meat and merry-making and much delight,
To such an extent that it would try me to tell of it,
Even if perhaps I made the effort to describe it.
But yet I know the knight and the nobly pretty one
Found such solace and satisfaction seated together,
In the discreet confidences of their courtly dalliance,
Their irreproachably pure and polished repartee,
That with princes' sport their play of wit surpassingly
  Compares.
 Pipes and side-drums sound,
 Trumpets entune their airs;
 Each soul its solace found,
 And the two were enthralled with theirs.

42

THAT day they made much merriment, and on the morrow again,
And thickly the joys thronged on the third day after;*
But gentle was the jubilation on St John's Day,
The final one for feasting, so the folk there thought.
As there were guests geared to go in the grey dawn
They watched the night out with wine in wonderful style,
Leaping night-long in their lordly dances.
At last when it was late those who lived far off,
Each one, bid farewell before wending their ways.
Gawain also said goodbye, but the good host grasped him,
Led him to the hearth of his own chamber,
And held him back hard, heartily thanking him
For the fine favour he had manifested to him
In honouring his house that high feast-tide,

Brightening his abode with his brilliant company:
'As long as I live, sir, I believe I shall thrive
Now Gawain has been my guest at God's own feast.'
'Great thanks, sir,' said Gawain. 'In good faith, yours,
All yours is the honour, may the High King requite it!
I stand at your service, knight, to satisfy your will
As good use engages me, in great things and small,
            By right.'
        The lord then bid his best
        Longer to delay the knight,
        But Gawain, replying, pressed
        His departure in all despite.

43

THEN with courteous inquiry the castellan asked
What fierce exploit had sent him forth, at that festive season,*
From the King's court at Camelot, so quickly and alone,
Before the holy time was over in the homes of men.
'You may in truth well demand,' admitted the knight.
'A high and urgent errand hastened me from thence,
For I myself am summoned to seek out a place
To find which I know not where in the world to look.
For all the land in Logres – may our Lord help me!*
I would not fail to find it on the feast of New Year.
So this is my suit, sir, which I beseech of you here,
That you tell me in truth if tale ever reached you
Of the Green Chapel, or what ground or glebe it stands on,
Or of the knight who holds it, whose hue is green.
For at that place I am pledged, by the pact between us,
To meet that man, if I remain alive.

From now until the New Year is not a great time,
And if God will grant it me, more gladly would I see him
Than gain any good possession, by God's son!
I must wend my way, with your good will, therefore;
I am reduced to three days in which to do my business,
And I think it fitter to fall dead than fail in my errand.'
Then the lord said laughingly, 'You may linger a while,
For I shall tell you where your tryst is by your term's end.
Give yourself no more grief for the Green Chapel's whereabouts,
For you may lie back in your bed, brave man, at ease*
Till full morning on the First, and then fare forth
To the meeting place at mid-morning to manage how you may
            Out there.
      Leave not till New Year's Day,
      Then get up and go with cheer;
      You shall be shown the way;
      It is hardly two miles from here.'

44

THEN Gawain was glad and gleefully exclaimed,
'Now above all, most heartily do I offer you thanks!
For my goal is now gained, and by grace of yours
I shall dwell here and do what you deem good for me.'
So the lord seized Sir Gawain, seated him beside himself,
And to enliven their delight, he had the ladies fetched,
And much gentle merriment they long made together.
The lord, as one like to take leave of his senses
And not aware of what he was doing, spoke warmly and merrily.
Then he spoke to Sir Gawain, saying out loud,
'You have determined to do the deed I ask:

61

Will you hold to your undertaking here and now?'
'Yes, sir, in good sooth,' said the true knight,
'While I stay in your stronghold, I shall stand at your command.'
'Since you have spurred,' the lord said, 'from afar,
Then watched awake with me, you are not well supplied
With either sustenance or sleep, for certain, I know;
So you shall lie long in your room, late and at ease
Tomorrow till the time of mass, and then take your meal
When you will, with my wife beside you
To comfort you with her company till I come back to court.

      You stay,
   And I shall get up at dawn.
   I will to the hunt away.'
   When Gawain's agreement was sworn
   He bowed, as brave knights may.

45

'MOREOVER,' said the man, 'Let us make a bargain*
That whatever I win in the woods be yours,
And any achievement you chance on here, you exchange for it.
Sweet sir, truly swear to such a bartering,
Whether fair fortune or foul befall from it.'
'By God,' said the good Gawain, 'I agree to that,
And I am happy that you have an eye to sport.'
Then the prince of that people said, 'What pledge of wine
Is brought to seal the bargain?' And they burst out laughing.
They took drink and toyed in trifling talk,
These lords and ladies, as long as they liked,
And then with French refinement and many fair words
They stood, softly speaking, to say goodnight,

Kissing as they parted company in courtly style.
With lithe liege servants in plenty and lambent torches,
Each brave man was brought to his bed at last,
   Full soft.
  Before they fared to bed
  They rehearsed their bargain oft.
  That people's prince, men said,
  Could fly his wit aloft.

FIT III

46

In the faint light before dawn folk were stirring;
Guests who had to go gave orders to their grooms,
Who busied themselves briskly with the beasts, saddling,
Trimming their tackle and tying on their luggage.
Arrayed for riding in the richest style,
Guests leaped on their mounts lightly, laid hold of their bridles,
And each rider rode out on his own chosen way.
The beloved lord of the land was not the last up,
Being arrayed for riding with his retinue in force.
He ate a sop hastily when he had heard mass,
And hurried with horn to the hunting field;
Before the sun's first rays fell on the earth,
On their high steeds were he and his knights.
Then these cunning hunters came to couple their hounds,
Cast open the kennel doors and called them out,
And blew on their bugles three bold notes.*
The hounds broke out barking, baying fiercely,
And when they went chasing, they were whipped back.
There were a hundred choice huntsmen there, whose fame
   Resounds.
  To their stations keepers strode;
  Huntsmen unleashed hounds:
  The forest overflowed
  With the strident bugle sounds.

47

AT the first cry wild creatures quivered with dread.
The deer in distraction darted down to the dales
Or up to the high ground, but eagerly they were
Driven back by the beaters, who bellowed lustily.
They let the harts with high-branching heads have their freedom,
And the brave bucks, too, with their broad antlers,
For the noble prince had expressly prohibited
Meddling with male deer in the months of close season.*
But the hinds were held back with a 'Hey' and a 'Whoa!'
And does driven with much din to the deep valleys.
Lo! the arrows' slanting flight as they were loosed!
A shaft flew forth at every forest turning,
The broad head biting on the brown flank.
They screamed as the blood streamed out, sank dead on the sward,
Always harried by hounds hard on their heels,
And the hurrying hunters' high horn notes.
Like the rending of ramped hills roared the din.
If one of the wild beasts slipped away from the archers
It was dragged down and met death at the dog-bases
After being hunted from the high ground and harried to the water,
So skilled were the hunt-servants at stations lower down,
So gigantic the greyhounds that grabbed them in a flash,
Seizing them savagely, as swift, I swear,
          As sight.
     The lord, in humour high
     Would spur, then stop and alight.
     In bliss the day went by
     Till dark drew on, and night.

65

48

THUS by the forest borders the brave lord sported,
And the good man Gawain, on his gay bed lying,★
Lay hidden till the light of day gleamed on the walls,
Covered with fair canopy, the curtains closed,
And as in slumber he slept on, there slipped into his mind
A slight, suspicious sound, and the door stealthily opened.
He raised up his head out of the bedclothes,
Caught up the corner of the curtain a little
And watched warily towards it, to see what it was.
It was the lady, loveliest to look upon,
Who secretly and silently secured the door,
Then bore towards his bed: the brave knight, embarrassed,
Lay flat with fine adroitness and feigned sleep.
Silently she stepped on, stole to his bed,
Caught up the curtain, crept within,
And seated herself softly on the side of the bed.
There she watched a long while, waiting for him to wake.
Slyly close this long while lay the knight,
Considering in his soul this circumstance,
Its sense and likely sequel, for it seemed marvellous.
'Still, it would be more circumspect,' he said to himself,
'To speak and discover her desire in due course.'
So he stirred and stretched himself, twisting towards her,
Opened his eyes and acted as if astounded;
And, to seem the safer by such service, crossed himself
   In dread.
  With chin and cheek so fair,
  White ranged with rosy red,
  With laughing lips, and air
  Of love, she lightly said:

49

'GOOD morning, Sir Gawain,' the gay one murmured,
'How unsafely you sleep, that one may slip in here!
Now you are taken in a trice. Unless a truce come between us,
I shall bind you to your bed – of that be sure.'
The lady uttered laughingly those playful words.
'Good morning, gay lady,' Gawain blithely greeted her.
'Do with me as you will: that well pleases me.
For I surrender speedily and sue for grace,
Which, to my mind, since I must, is much the best course.'
And thus he repaid her with repartee and ready laughter.
'But if, lovely lady, your leave were forthcoming,
And you were pleased to free your prisoner and pray him to rise,
I would abandon my bed for a better habiliment,
And have more happiness in our honey talk.'
'Nay, verily, fine sir,' urged the voice of that sweet one,
'You shall not budge from your bed. I have a better idea.
I shall hold you fast here on this other side as well
And so chat on with the chevalier my chains have caught.
For I know well, my knight, that your name is Sir Gawain,
Whom all the world worships, wherever he ride;
For lords and their ladies, and all living folk,
Hold your honour in high esteem, and your courtesy.
And now – here you are truly, and we are utterly alone;
My lord and his liegemen are a long way off;
Others still bide in their beds, my bower-maidens too;
Shut fast and firmly with a fine hasp is the door;
And since I have in this house him who pleases all,
As long as my time lasts I shall lingering in talk take
        My fill.

My young body is yours,★
Do with it what you will;
My strong necessities force
Me to be your servant still.'

50

'IN good truth,' said Gawain, 'that is a gain indeed,
Though I am hardly the hero of whom you speak.
To be held in such honour as you here suggest,
I am altogether unworthy, I own it freely.
By God, I should be glad ,if you granted it right
For me to essay by speech or some other service,
To pleasure such a perfect lady – pure joy it would be.'
'In good truth, Sir Gawain,' the gay lady replied,
'If I slighted or set at naught your spotless fame
And your all-pleasing prowess, it would show poor breeding.
But there is no lack of ladies who would love, noble one,
To hold you in their arms, as I have you here,
And linger in the luxury of your delightful discourse,
Which would perfectly pleasure them and appease their woes –
Rather than have riches or the red gold they own.
But as I love that Lord, the Celestial Ruler,
I have wholly in my hand what all desire
                Through his grace.'
        Not loth was she to allure,
        This lady fair of face;
        But the knight with speeches pure
        Answered in each case.

Respects the women!

51

'MADAM,' said the merry man, 'May Mary requite you!
For in good faith I have found in you free-hearted generosity.
Certain men for their deeds receive esteem from others,
But for myself, I do not deserve the respect they show me;
Your honourable mind makes you utter only what is good.'
'Now by Mary,' said the noble lady, 'Not so it seems to me,
For were I worth the whole of womankind,
And all the wealth in the world were in my hand,
And if bargaining I were to bid to bring myself a lord –
With your noble qualities, knight, made known to me now,
Your good looks, gracious manner and great courtesy,
All of which I have heard of before, but here prove true –
No lord that is living could be allowed to excel you.'
'Indeed, dear lady, you did better,' said the knight,*
'But I am proud of the precious price you put on me,
And solemnly as your servant say you are my sovereign.
May Christ requite it you: I have become your knight.'
Then of many matters they talked till mid-morning and after,
And all the time she behaved as if she adored him;
But Sir Gawain was on guard in a gracious manner.
Though she was the winsomest woman the warrior had known,*
He was less love-laden because of the loss he must
            Now face –
      His destruction by the stroke,
      For come it must was the case.
      The lady of leaving then spoke;
      He assented with speedy grace.

2 hunts going on

52

THEN she gave him goodbye, glinting with laughter,
And standing up, astounded him with these strong words:
'May He who prospers every speech for this pleasure reward you!
I cannot bring myself to believe that you could be Gawain.'
'How so?' said the knight, speaking urgently,
For he feared he had failed to observe the forms of courtesy.
But the beauteous one blessed him and brought out this argument:
'Such a great man as Gawain is granted to be,
The very vessel of virtue and fine courtesy,
Could scarcely have stayed such a sojourn with a lady
Without craving a kiss out of courtesy,
Touched by some trifling hint at the tail-end of a speech.'
'So be it, as you say,' then said Gawain,
'I shall kiss at your command, as becomes a knight
Who fears to offend you; no further plea is needed.'
Whereupon she approached him, and penned him in her arms,
Leaned over him lovingly and gave the lord a kiss.
Then they commended each other to Christ in comely style,
And without more words she went out by the door.
He made ready to rise with rapid haste,
Summoned his servant, selected his garb,
And walked down, when he was dressed, debonairly to mass.
Then he went to the well-served meal which awaited him,
And made merry sport till the moon rose
        At night.
    Never was baron bold
    So taken by ladies bright,
    That young one and the old:
    They throve all three in delight.

70

COURTLY LOVE

53

KNIFE

AND still at his sport spurred the castellan,
Hunting the barren hinds in holt and on heath.
So many had he slain, by the setting of the sun,
Of does and other deer, that it was downright wonderful.
Then at the finish the folk flocked in eagerly,
And quickly collected the killed deer in a heap.
Those highest in rank came up with hosts of attendants,*
Picked out what appeared to be the plumpest beasts
And, according to custom, had them cut open with finesse.
Some who ceremoniously assessed them there
Found two fingers' breadth of fat on the worst.
Then they slit open the slot, seized the first stomach,
Scraped it with a keen knife and tied up the tripes.
Next they hacked off all the legs, the hide was stripped,
The belly broken open and the bowels removed
Carefully, lest they loosen the ligature of the knot.
Then they gripped the gullet, disengaged deftly
The wezand from the windpipe and whipped out the guts.
Then their sharp knives shore through the shoulder-bones,
Which they slid out of a small hole, leaving the sides intact.
Then they cleft the chest clean through, cutting it in two.
Then again at the gullet a man began to work
And straight away rived it, right to the fork,
Flicked out the shoulder-fillets, and faithfully then
He rapidly ripped free the rib-fillets.
Similarly, as is seemly, the spine was cleared
All the way to the haunch, which hung from it;
And they heaved up the whole haunch and hewed it off;

And that is called, according to its kind, the numbles,★
     I find.
    At the thigh-forks then they strain
    And free the folds behind,
    Hurrying to hack all in twain,
    The backbone to unbind.

54

THEN they hewed off the head and also the neck,
And after sundered the sides swiftly from the chine,
And into the foliage they flung the fee of the raven.★
Then each fellow, for his fee, as it fell to him to have,
Skewered through the stout flanks beside the ribs,
And then by the hocks of the haunches they hung up their booty.
On one of the finest fells they fed their hounds,
And let them have the lights, the liver and the tripes,
With bread well imbrued with blood mixed with them.
Boldly they blew the kill amid the baying of hounds.
Then off they went homewards, holding their meat,
Stalwartly sounding many stout horn-calls.
As dark was descending, they were drawing near
To the comely castle where quietly our knight stayed.
     Fires roared,
    And blithely hearts were beating
    As into hall came the lord.
    When Gawain gave him greeting,
    Joy abounded at the board.

55

THEN the master commanded everyone to meet in the hall,
Called the ladies to come down with their company of maidens.
Before all the folk on the floor, he bid men
Fetch the venison and place it before him.
Then gaily and in good humour to Gawain he called,
Told over the tally of the sturdy beasts,
And showed him the fine fat flesh flayed from the ribs.
'How does the sport please you? Do you praise me for it?
Am I thoroughly thanked for thriving as a huntsman?'
'Certainly,' said the other, 'Such splendid spoils
Have I not seen for seven years in the season of winter.'
'And I give you all, Gawain,' said the good man then,
'For according to our covenant you may claim it as your own.'
'Certes, that is so, and I say the same to you,'
Said Gawain, 'For my true gains in this great house,
I am not loth to allow, must belong to you.'
And he put his arms round his handsome neck, hugging him,★
And kissed him in the comeliest way he could think of.
'Accept my takings, sir, for I received no more;
Gladly would I grant them, however great they were.'
'And therefore I thank you,' the thane said, 'Good!
Yours may be the better gift, if you would break it to me
Where your wisdom won you wealth of that kind.'
'No such clause in our contract! Request nothing else!'
Said the other, 'You have your due: ask more,
　　　None should.'
　　They laughed in blithe assent
　　With worthy words and good;

Then to supper they swiftly went,
To fresh delicious food.

56

AND sitting afterwards by the hearth of an audience chamber,
Where retainers repeatedly brought them rare wines,
In their jolly jesting they jointly agreed
On a settlement similar to the preceding one;
To exchange the chance achievements of the morrow,
No matter how novel they were, at night when they met.
They accorded on this compact, the whole court observing,
And the bumper was brought forth in banter to seal it.
And at last they lovingly took leave of each other,
Each man hastening thereafter to his bed.
The cock having crowed and called only thrice,★
The lord leaped from bed, and his liegemen too,
So that mass and a meal were meetly dealt with,
And by first light the folk to the forest were bound
        For the chase.
    Proudly the hunt with horns
    Soon drove through a desert place:
    Uncoupled through the thorns
    The great hounds pressed apace.

57

By a quagmire they quickly scented quarry and gave tongue,★
And the chief huntsman urged on the first hounds up,
Spurring them on with a splendid spate of words.★
The hounds, hearing it, hurried there at once,

Fell on the trial furiously, forty together,
And made such echoing uproar, all howling at once,
That the rocky banks round about rang with the din.
Hunters inspirited them with sound of speech and horn.
Then together in a group, across the ground they surged
At speed between a pool and a spiteful crag.
On a stony knoll by a steep cliff at the side of a bog,
Where rugged rocks had roughly tumbled down,
They careered on the quest, the cry following,
Then surrounded the crag and the rocky knoll as well,
Certain their prey skulked inside their ring,
For the baying of the bloodhounds meant the beast was there.
Then they beat upon the bushes and bade him come out,
And he swung out savagely aslant the line of men,
A baneful boar of unbelievable size,
A solitary long since sundered from the herd,
Being old and brawny, the biggest of them all,
And grim and ghastly when he grunted: great was the grief
When he thrust through the hounds, hurling three to earth,
And sped on scot-free, swift and unscathed.
They hallooed, yelled, 'Look out!' cried, 'Hey, we have him!'
And blew horns boldly, to bring the bloodhounds together;
Many were the merry cries from men and dogs
As they hurried clamouring after their quarry to kill him on
          The track.
      Many times he turns at bay
      And tears the dogs which attack.
      He hurts the hounds, and they
      Moan in a piteous pack.

58

Then men shoved forward, shaped to shoot at him,
Loosed arrows at him, hitting him often,
But the points, for all their power, could not pierce his flanks,
Nor would the barbs bite on his bristling brow.*
Though the smooth-shaven shaft shattered in pieces,
Wherever it hit, the head rebounded.
But when the boar was battered by blows unceasing,
Goaded and driven demented, he dashed at the men,
Striking them savagely as he assailed them in rushes,
So that some lacking stomach stood back in fear.
But the lord on a lithe horse lunged after him,
Blew on his bugle like a bold knight in battle,
Rallied the hounds as he rode through the rank thickets,
Pursuing this savage boar till the sun set.
And so they disported themselves this day
While our lovable lord lay in his bed.
At home the gracious Gawain in gorgeous clothes
    Reclined:
      The gay one did not forget
      To come with welcome kind,
      And early him beset
      To make him change his mind.

59

SHE came to the curtain and cast her eye
On Sir Gawain, who at once gave her gracious welcome,
And she answered him eagerly, with ardent words,
Sat at his side softly, and with a spurt of laughter

And a loving look, delivered these words:
'It seems to me strange, if, sir, you are Gawain,
A person so powerfully disposed to good,
Yet nevertheless know nothing of noble conventions,
And when made aware of them, wave them away!
Quickly you have cast off what I schooled you in yesterday
By the truest of all tokens of talk I know of.'
'What?' said the wondering knight, 'I am not aware of one.
But if it be true what you tell, I am entirely to blame.'
'I counselled you then about kissing,' the comely one said;
'When a favour is conferred, it must be forthwith accepted:
That is becoming for a courtly knight who keeps the rules.'
'Sweet one, unsay that speech,' said the brave man,
'For I dared not do that lest I be denied.
If I were forward and were refused, the fault would be mine.'
'But none,' said the noblewoman, 'could deny you, by my faith!
You are strong enough to constrain with your strength if you wish,
If any were so ill-bred as to offer you resistance.'
'Yes, good guidance you give me, by God,' replied Gawain,
'But threateners are ill thought of and do not thrive in my country,
Nor do gifts thrive when given without good will.
I am here at your behest, to offer a kiss to when you like;
You may do it whenever you deem fit, or desist,
          In this place.'
     The beautiful lady bent
     And fairly kissed his face;
     Much speech the two then spent
     On love, its grief and grace.

60

'I WOULD know of you, knight,' the noble lady said,
'If it did not anger you, what argument you use,
Being so hale and hearty as you are at this time,
So generous a gentleman as you are justly famed to be;
Since the choicest thing in Chivalry, the chief thing praised,
Is the loyal sport of love, the very lore of arms?
For the tale of the contentions of true knights
Is told by the title and text of their feats,
How lords for their true loves put their lives at hazard,
Endured dreadful trials for their dear loves' sakes,
And with valour avenged and made void their woes,
Bringing home abundant bliss by their virtues.
You are the gentlest and most just of your generation;
Everywhere your honour and high fame are known;
Yet I have sat at your side two separate times here
Without hearing you utter in any way
A single syllable of the saga of love.
Being so polished and punctilious a pledge-fulfiller,
You ought to be eager to lay open to a young thing
Your discoveries in the craft of courtly love.
What! Are you ignorant, with all your renown?
Or do you deem me too dull to drink in your dalliance?
            For shame!
    I sit here unchaperoned, and stay
    To acquire some courtly game;
    So while my lord is away,
    Teach me your true wit's fame.'

61

'IN good faith,' said Gawain, 'may God requite you!
It gives me great happiness, and is good sport to me,
That so fine a fair one as you should find her way here
And take pains with so poor a man, make pastime with her knight,
With any kind of clemency – it comforts me greatly.
But for me to take on the travail of interpreting true love
And construing the subjects of the stories of arms
To you who, I hold, have more skill
In that art, by half, than a hundred of such
As I am or ever shall be on the earth I inhabit,
Would in faith be a manifold folly, noble lady.
To please you I would press with all the power in my soul,
For I am highly beholden to you, and evermore shall be
True servant to your bounteous self, so save me God!'
So that stately lady tempted him and tried him with questions
To win him to wickedness, whatever else she thought.*
But he defended himself so firmly that no fault appeared,
Nor was there any evil apparent on either side,
    But bliss;
    For long they laughed and played
    Till she gave him a gracious kiss.
    A fond farewell she bade,
    And went her way on this.

62

SIR Gawain bestirred himself and went to mass:
Then dinner was dressed and with due honour served.
All day long the lord and the ladies disported,

But the castellan coursed across the country time and again,
Hunted his hapless boar as it hurtled over the hills,
Then bit the backs of his best hounds asunder
Standing at bay, till the bowmen obliged him to break free
Out into the open for all he could do,
So fast the arrows flew when the folk there concentrated.
Even the strongest he sometimes made start back,
But in time he became so tired he could tear away no more,
And with the speed he still possessed, he spurted to a hole
On a rise by a rock with a running stream beside.
He got the bank at his back, and began to abrade the ground.
The froth was foaming foully at his mouth,
And he whetted his white tusks; a weary time it was
For the bold men about, who were bound to harass him
From a distance, for none dared to draw near him
　　　　For dread.
　　　He had hurt so many men
　　　That it entered no one's head
　　　To be torn by his tusks again,
　　　And he raging and seeing red.

63

TILL the castellan came himself, encouraging his horse,
And saw the boar at bay with his band of men around.
He alighted in lively fashion, left his courser,
Drew and brandished his bright sword and boldly strode forward,*
Striding at speed through the stream to where the savage beast was.
The wild thing was aware of the weapon and its wielder,
And so bridled with its bristles in a burst of fierce snorts
That all were anxious for the lord, lest he have the worst of it.

Straight away the savage brute sprang at the man,
And baron and boar were both in a heap
In the swirling water: the worst went to the beast,
For the man had marked him well at the moment of impact,
Had put the point precisely at the pit of his chest,
And drove it in to the hilt, so that the heart was shattered,
And the spent beast sank snarling and was swept downstream,
        Teeth bare.
    A hundred hounds and more
    Attack and seize and tear;
    Men tug him to the shore
    And the dogs destroy him there.

64

BUGLES blew the triumph, horns blared loud.
There was hallooing in high pride by all present;
Braches bayed at the beast, as bidden by their masters,
The chief huntsmen in charge of that chase so hard.
Then one who was wise in wood-crafts
Started in style to slash open the boar.
First he hewed off the head and hoisted it on high,
Then rent him roughly along the ridge of his back,
Brought out the bowels and broiled them on coals
For blending with bread as the braches' reward.
Then he broke out the brawn from the bright broad flanks,
Took out the offal, as is fit,
Attached the two halves entirely together,
And on a strong stake stoutly hung them.
Then home they hurried with the huge beast,
With the boar's head borne before the baron himself,

Who had destroyed him in the stream by the strength of his arm,
>   Above all:
>   It seemed to him an age
>   Till he greeted Gawain in hall.
>   To reap his rightful wage
>   The latter came at his call.

65

THE lord exclaimed loudly, laughing merrily
When he saw Sir Gawain, and spoke joyously.
The sweet ladies were sent for, and the servants assembled.
Then he showed them the shields, and surely described★
The large size and length, and the malignity
Of the fierce boar's fighting when he fled in the woods;
So that Gawain congratulated him on his great deed,
Commended it as a merit he had manifested well,
For a beast with so much brawn, the bold man said,
A boar of such breadth, he had not before seen.
When they handled the huge head the upright man praised it,
Expressed horror thereat for the ear of the lord.
'Now Gawain,' said the good man, 'this game is your own
By our contracted treaty, in truth, you know.'
'It is so,' said the knight, 'and as certainly
I shall give you all my gains as guerdon, in faith.'
He clasped the castellan's neck and kissed him kindly,
And then served him a second time in the same style.
'In all our transactions since I came to sojourn,' asserted Gawain,
'Up to tonight, as of now, there's nothing that
>   I owe.'
>   'By Saint Giles,' the castellan quipped,★

82

'You're the finest fellow I know:
Your wealth will have us whipped
If your trade continues so!'*

66

THEN the trestles and tables were trimly set out,
Complete with cloths, and clearly flaming cressets
And waxen torches were placed in the wall-brackets
By retainers, who then tended the entire hall-gathering.
Much gladness and glee then gushed forth there
By the fire on the floor: and in multifarious ways
They sang noble songs at supper and afterwards,
A concert of Christmas carols and new dance songs,*
With the most mannerly mirth a man could tell of,
And our courteous knight kept constant company with the lady.
In a bewitchingly well-mannered way she made up to him,
Secretly soliciting the stalwart knight
So that he was astounded, and upset in himself.
But his upbringing forbade him to rebuff her utterly,
So he behaved towards her honourably, whatever aspersions might
        Be cast.
    They revelled in the hall
    As long as their pleasure might last
    And then at the castellan's call
    To the chamber hearth they passed.

67

THERE they drank and discoursed and decided to enjoy
Similar solace and sport on New Year's Eve.

But the princely knight asked permission to depart in the morning,
For his appointed time was approaching, and perforce he must go.
But the lord would not let him and implored him to linger,
Saying, 'I swear to you, as a staunch true knight,
You shall gain the Green Chapel to give your dues,
My lord, in the light of New Year, long before sunrise.
Therefore remain in your room and rest in comfort,
While I fare hunting in the forest; in fulfilment of our oath
Exchanging what we achieve when the chase is over.
For twice I have tested you, and twice found you true.*
Now "Third time, throw best!" Think of that tomorrow!
Let us make merry while we may, set our minds on joy,
For hard fate can hit man whenever it likes.'
This was graciously granted and Gawain stayed.
Blithely drink was brought, then to bed with lights
          They pressed.
      All night Sir Gawain sleeps
      Softly and still at rest;
      But the lord his custom keeps
      And is early up and dressed.

68

AFTER mass, he and his men made a small meal.
Merry was the morning; he demanded his horse.
The men were ready mounted before the main gate,
A host of knightly horsemen to follow after him.
Wonderfully fair was the forest-land, for the frost remained,
And the rising sun shone ruddily on the ragged clouds,
In its beauty brushing their blackness off the heavens.
The huntsmen unleashed the hounds by a holt-side,

And the rocks and surrounding bushes rang with their horn-calls.
Some found and followed the fox's tracks,★
And wove various ways in their wily fashion.
A small hound cried the scent, the senior huntsman called
His fellow foxhounds to him and, feverishly sniffing,★
The rout of dogs rushed forward on the right path.
The fox hurried fast, for they found him soon
And, seeing him distinctly, pursued him at speed,
Unmistakably giving tongue with tumultuous din.
Deviously in difficult country he doubled on his tracks,
Swerved and wheeled away, often waited listening,
Till at last by a little ditch he leaped a quickset hedge,
And stole out stealthily at the side of a valley,
Considering his stratagem had given the slip to the hounds.
But he stumbled on a tracking-dogs' tryst-place unawares,
And there in a cleft three hounds threatened him at once,

     All grey.
  He swiftly started back,
  And, full of deep dismay,
  He dashed on a different track;
  To the woods he went away.

69

THEN came the lively delight of listening to hounds
When they had all met in a muster, mingling together,
For, catching sight of him, they cried such curses on him
That the clustering cliffs seemed to be crashing down.
Here he was hallooed when the hunters met him,
There savagely snarled at by intercepting hounds;
Then he was called thief and threatened often;

With the tracking dogs on his tail, no tarrying was possible.
When out in the open he was often run at,
So he often swerved in again, that artful Reynard.
Yes, he led the lord and his liegemen a dance
In this manner among the mountains till mid-afternoon,
While harmoniously at home the honoured knight slept
Between the comely curtains in the cold morning.
But the lady's longing to woo would not let her sleep,*
Nor would she impair the purpose pitched in her heart,
But rose up rapidly and ran to him
In a ravishing robe that reached to the ground,
Trimmed with finest fur from pure pelts;
Not coifed as to custom, but with costly jewels
Strung in scores on her splendid hairnet.
Her fine-featured face and fair throat were unveiled,
Her breast was bare and her back as well.
She came in by the chamber door and closed it after her,
Cast open a casement and called on the knight,
And briskly thus rebuked him with bountiful words
         Of good cheer.
    'Ah sir! What, sound asleep?
    The morning's crisp and clear.'
    He had been drowsing deep,
    But now he had to hear.

                70

THE noble sighed ceaselessly in unsettled slumber
As threatening thoughts thronged in the dawn light
About destiny, which the day after would deal him his fate
At the Green Chapel where Gawain was to greet his man,

And be bound to bear his buffet unresisting.
But having recovered consciousness in comely fashion,
He heaved himself out of dreams and answered hurriedly.
The lovely lady advanced, laughing adorably,
Swooped over his splendid face and sweetly kissed him.
He welcomed her worthily with noble cheer
And, gazing on her gay and glorious attire,
Her features so faultless and fine of complexion,
He felt a flush of rapture suffuse his heart.★
Sweet and genial smiling slid them into joy
Till bliss burst forth between them, beaming gay
  And bright;
  With joy the two contended
  In talk of true delight,
  And peril would have impended
  Had Mary not minded her knight.

71

FOR that peerless princess pressed him so hotly,★
So invited him to the very verge, that he felt forced
Either to allow her love or blackguardly rebuff her.
He was concerned for his courtesy, lest he be called caitiff,
But more especially for his evil plight if he should plunge into sin,
And dishonour the owner of the house treacherously.
'God shield me! That shall not happen, for sure,' said the knight.
So with laughing love-talk he deflected gently
The downright declarations that dropped from her lips.
Said the beauty to the bold man, 'Blame will be yours
If you love not the living body lying close to you
More than all wooers in the world who are wounded in heart;

Unless you have a lover more beloved, who delights you more,
A maiden to whom you are committed, so immutably bound
That you do not seek to sever from her – which I see is so.
Tell me the truth of it, I entreat you now;
By all the loves there are, do not hide the truth
      With guile.'
    Then gently, 'By Saint John,'*
    Said the knight with a smile,
    'I owe my oath to none,
    Nor wish to yet a while.'

72

'THOSE words,' said the fair woman, 'are the worst there could be,
But I am truly answered, to my utter anguish.
Give me now a gracious kiss, and I shall go from here
As a maid that loves much, mourning on this earth.'
Then, sighing, she stooped, and seemlily kissed him,
And, severing herself from him, stood up and said,
'At this adieu, my dear one, do me this pleasure:
Give me something as gift, your glove if no more,
To mitigate my mourning when I remember you.'
'Now certainly, for your sake,' said the knight,
'I wish I had here the handsomest thing I own,
For you have deserved, forsooth, superabundantly
And rightfully, a richer reward than I could give.
But as tokens of true love, trifles mean little.
It is not to your honour to have at this time
A mere glove as Gawain's gift to treasure.
For I am here on an errand in unknown regions,
And have no bondsmen, no baggages with dear-bought things in them.

This afflicts me now, fair lady, for your sake.
Man must do as he must; neither lament it
        Nor repine.'
    'No, highly honoured one,'
    Replied that lady fine,
    'Though gift you give me none,
    You must have something of mine.'

73

SHE proffered him a rich ring wrought in red gold,
With a sparkling stone set conspicuously in it,
Which beamed as brilliantly as the bright sun;
You may well believe its worth was wonderfully great.
But the courteous man declined it and quickly said,
'Before God, gracious lady, no giving just now!
Not having anything to offer, I shall accept nothing.'
She offered it him urgently and he refused again,
Fast affirming his refusal on his faith as a knight.
Put out by this repulse, she presently said,
'If you reject my ring as too rich in value,
Doubtless you would be less deeply indebted to me
If I gave you my girdle, a less gainful gift.'
She swiftly slipped off the cincture of her gown
Which went round her waist under the wonderful mantle,
A girdle of green silk with a golden hem,
Embroidered only at the edges, with hand-stitched ornament.
And she pleaded with the prince in a pleasant manner
To take it notwithstanding its trifling worth;
But he told her that he could touch no treasure at all,
Not gold nor any gift, till God gave him grace

To pursue to success the search he was bound on.
'And therefore I beg you not to be displeased:
Press no more your purpose, for I promise it never
          Can be.
      I owe you a hundredfold
      For grace you have granted me;
      And ever through hot and cold
      I shall stay your devotee.'

74

'Do you say "no" to this silk?' then said the beauty,
'Because it is simple in itself? And so it seems.
Lo! It is little indeed, and so less worth your esteem.
But one who was aware of the worth twined in it★
Would appraise its properties as more precious perhaps,
For the man that binds his body with this belt of green,
As long as he laps it closely about him,
No hero under heaven can hack him to pieces,
For he cannot be killed by any cunning on earth.'
Then the prince pondered, and it appeared to him
A precious gem to protect him in the peril appointed him
When he gained the Green Chapel to be given checkmate:
It would be a splendid stratagem to escape being slain.
Then he allowed her to solicit him and let her speak.
She pressed the belt upon him with potent words
And having got his agreement, she gave it him gladly,
Beseeching him for her sake to conceal it always,
And hide it from her husband with all diligence.
That never should another know of it, the noble swore★
          Outright.

Then often his thanks gave he
With all his heart and might,
And thrice by then had she
Kissed the constant knight.

75

THEN with a word of farewell she went away,
For she could not force further satisfaction from him.
Directly she withdrew, Sir Gawain dressed himself,
Rose and arrayed himself in rich garments,
But laid aside the love-lace the lady had given him,
Secreted it carefully where he could discover it later.
Then he went his way at once to the chapel,*
Privily approached a priest and prayed him there
To listen to his life's sins and enlighten him
On how he might have salvation in the hereafter.
Then, confessing his faults, he fairly shrove himself,
Begging mercy for both major and minor sins.
He asked the holy man for absolution
And was absolved with certainty and sent out so pure*
That Doomsday could have been declared the day after.
Then he made merrier among the noble ladies,
With comely carolling and all kinds of pleasure,
Than ever he had done, with ecstasy, till came
          Dark night.
     Such honour he did to all,
     They said, 'Never has this knight
     Since coming into hall
     Expressed such pure delight.'

76

Now long may he linger there, love sheltering him!*
The prince was still on the plain, pleasuring in the chase,
Having finished off the fox he had followed so far.
As he leaped over a hedge looking out for the quarry,
Where he heard the hounds that were harrying the fox,
Reynard came running through a rough thicket
With the pack all pell-mell, panting at his heels.
The lord, aware of the wild beast, waited craftily,
Then drew his dazzling sword and drove at the fox.
The beast baulked at the blade to break sideways,
But a dog bounded at him before he could,
And right in front of the horse's feet they fell on him,
All worrying their wily prey with a wild uproar.
The lord quickly alighted and lifted him up,
Wrenched him beyond reach of the ravening fangs,
Held him high over his head and hallooed lustily,
While the angry hounds in hordes bayed at him.
Thither hurried the huntsmen with horns in plenty,
Sounding the rally splendidly till they saw their lord.
When the company of his court had come up to the kill,
All who bore bugles blew at once,
And the others without horns hallooed loudly.
The requiem that was raised for Reynard's soul
And the commotion made it the merriest meet ever,
     Men said.
    The hounds must have their fee:
    They pat them on the head,
    Then hold the fox; and he
    Is reft of his skin of red.

77

THEN they set off for home, it being almost night,
Blowing their big horns bravely as they went.
At last the lord alighted at his beloved castle
And found upon the floor a fire, and beside it
The good Sir Gawain in a glad humour
By reason of the rich friendship he had reaped from the ladies.
He wore a turquoise tunic extending to the ground;*
His softly-furred surcoat suited him well,
And his hood of the same hue hung from his shoulder.
All trimmed with ermine were hood and surcoat.
Meeting the master in the middle of the floor,
Gawain went forward gladly and greeted him thus:
'Forthwith, I shall be the first to fulfil the contract*
We settled so suitably without sparing the wine.'
Then he clasped the castellan and kissed him thrice
As sweetly and steadily as a strong knight could.
'By Christ!' quoth the other, 'You will carve yourself a fortune
By traffic in this trade when the terms suit you!'
'Do not chop logic about the exchange,' chipped in Gawain,
'As I have properly paid over the profit I made.'
'Marry,' said the other man, 'Mine is inferior,
For I have hunted all day and have only taken
This ill-favoured fox's skin, may the Fiend take it!
And that is a poor price to pay for such precious things
As you have pressed upon me here, three pure kisses
     So good.'
      'Enough!' acknowledged Gawain,
      'I thank you, by the Rood.'
     And how the fox was slain
     The lord told him as they stood.*

78

WITH mirth and minstrelsy, and meals when they liked,
They made as merry then as ever men could;
With the laughter of ladies and delightful jesting,
Gawain and his good host were very gay together,
Save when excess or sottishness seemed likely.
Master and men made many a witty sally,
Until presently, at the appointed parting-time,
The brave men were bidden to bed at last.
Then of his host the hero humbly took leave,
The first to bid farewell, fairly thanking him:
'May the High King requite you for your courtesy at this feast,
And the wonderful week of my dwelling here!
I would offer to be one of your own men if you liked,
But that I must move on tomorrow, as you know,
If you will give me the guide you granted me,
To show me the Green Chapel where my share of doom
Will be dealt on New Year's Day, as God deems for me.'
'With all my heart!' said the host. 'In good faith,
All that I ever promised you, I shall perform.'*
He assigned him a servant to set him on his way,
And lead him in the hills without any delay,
Faring through forest and thicket by the most straightforward route
      They might.
   With every honour due
   Gawain then thanked the knight,
   And having bid him adieu,
   Took leave of the ladies bright.

79

So he spoke to them sadly, sorrowing as he kissed,
And urged on them heartily his endless thanks,
And they gave to Sir Gawain words of grace in return,
Commending him to Christ with cries of chill sadness.
Then from the whole household he honourably took his leave,
Making all the men that he met amends
For their several services and solicitous care,
For they had been busily attendant, bustling about him;
And every soul was as sad to say farewell
As if they had always had the hero in their house.
Then the lords led him with lights to his chamber,
And blithely brought him to bed to rest.
If he slept – I dare not assert it – less soundly than usual,
There was much on his mind for the morrow, if he meant to give
　　　　It thought.
　　Let him lie there still,
　　He almost has what he sought;
　　So tarry a while until
　　The process I report.

FIT IV

80

Now the New Year neared, the night passed,
Daylight fought darkness as the Deity ordained.
But wild was the weather the world awoke to;
Bitterly the clouds cast down cold on the earth,
Inflicting on the flesh flails from the north.
Bleakly the snow blustered, and beasts were frozen;
The whistling wind wailed from the heights,
Driving great drifts deep in the dales.
Keenly the lord listened as he lay in his bed;
Though his lids were closed, he was sleeping little.
Every cock that crew recalled to him his tryst.*
Before the day had dawned, he had dressed himself,
For the light from a lamp illuminated his chamber.
He summoned his servant, who swiftly answered,
Commanded that his mail-coat and mount's saddle he brought.
The man fared forth and fetched him his armour,
And set Sir Gawain's array in splendid style.
First he clad him in his clothes to counter the cold,
Then in his other armour which had been well kept;
His breast- and belly-armour had been burnished bright,
And the rusty rings of his rich mail-coat rolled clean,*
And all being as fresh as at first, he was fain to give thanks
            Indeed.
      Each wiped and polished piece
      He donned with due heed.
      The gayest from here to Greece,
      The strong man sent for his steed.

96

81

WHILE he was putting on apparel of the most princely kind –
His surcoat, with its symbol of spotless deeds
Environed on velvet with virtuous gems,
Was embellished and bound with embroidered seams,
And finely fur-lined with the fairest skins –
He did not leave the lace belt, the lady's gift:
For his own good, Gawain did not forget that!
When he had strapped the sword on his swelling hips,
The knight lapped his loins with his love-token twice,
Quickly wrapped it with relish round his waist.
The green silken girdle suited the gallant well,
Backed by the royal red cloth that richly showed.
But Gawain wore the girdle not for its great value,
Nor through pride in the pendants, in spite of their polish,
Nor for the gleaming gold which glinted on the ends,
But to save himself when of necessity he must
Stand an evil stroke, not resisting it with knife
          Or sword.
     When ready and robed aright,
     Out came the comely lord;
     To the men of name and might
     His thanks in plenty poured.

82

Then was Gringolet got ready, that great huge horse.
Having been assiduously stabled in seemly quarters,
The fiery steed was fit and fretting for a gallop.
Sir Gawain stepped to him and, inspecting his coat,
Said earnestly to himself, asserting with truth,

'Here in this castle is a company whose conduct is honourable.
The man who maintains them, may he have joy!
The delightful lady, love befall her while she lives!
Thus for charity they cherish a chance guest
Honourably and open-handedly; may He on high,
The King of Heaven, requite you and your company too!
And if I could live any longer in lands on earth,
Some rich recompense, if I could, I should readily give you.'
Then he stepped into the stirrup and swung aloft.
His man showed him his shield; on his shoulder he put it,★
And gave the spur to Gringolet with his gold-spiked heels.
The horse sprang forward from the paving, pausing no more
      To prance.
    His man was mounted and fit,
    Laden with spear and lance.
    'This castle to Christ I commit:
    May He its fortune enhance!'

83

THE drawbridge was let down and the broad double gates
Were unbarred and borne open on both sides.
Passing over the planks, the prince blessed himself
And praised the kneeling porter, who proffered him 'Good day',
Praying God to grant that Gawain would be saved.
And Gawain went on his way with the one man★
To put him on the right path for that perilous place
Where the sad assault must be received by him.
By bluffs where boughs were bare they passed,
Climbed by cliffs where the cold clung:
Under the high clouds, ugly mists

Merged damply with the moors and melted on the mountains;
Each hill had a hat, a huge mantle of mist.
Brooks burst forth above them, boiling over their banks
And showering down sharply in shimmering cascades.
Wonderfully wild was their way through the woods;
Till soon the sun in the sway of that season

        Brought day.
    They were on a lofty hill
    Where snow beside them lay,
    When the servant stopped still
    And told his master to stay.

84

'For I have guided you to this ground, Sir Gawain, at this time,
And now you are not far from the noted place
Which you have searched for and sought with such special zeal.
But I must say to you, forsooth, since I know you,
And you are a lord whom I love with no little regard:
Take my governance as guide, and it shall go better for you,
For the place is perilous that you are pressing towards.
In that wilderness dwells the worst man in the world,
For he is valiant and fierce and fond of fighting,
And mightier than any man that may be on earth,
And his body is bigger than the best four
In Arthur's house, or Hector, or any other.
At the Green Chapel he gains his great adventures.
No man passes that place, however proud in arms,
Without being dealt a death-blow by his dreadful hand.
For he is an immoderate man, to mercy a stranger;*
For whether churl or chaplain by the chapel rides,

Monk or mass-priest or man of other kind,
He thinks it as convenient to kill him as keep alive himself.
Therefore I say, as certainly as you sit in your saddle,
If you come there you'll be killed, I caution you, knight,
Take my troth for it, though you had twenty lives
   And more.
  He has lived here since long ago
  And filled the field with gore.
  You cannot counter his blow,
  It strikes so sudden and sore.

85

'THEREFORE, good Sir Gawain, leave the grim man alone!
Ride by another route, to some region remote!
Go in the name of God, and Christ grace your fortune!
And I shall go home again and undertake
To swear solemnly by God and his saints as well
(By my halidom, so help me God, and every other oath)
Stoutly to keep your secret, not saying to a soul
That ever you tried to turn tail from any man I knew.'
'Great thanks,' replied Gawain, somewhat galled, and said,
'It is worthy of you to wish for my well-being, man,
And I believe you would loyally lock it in your heart.
But however quiet you kept it, if I quit this place,
Fled from the fellow in the fashion you propose,
I should become a cowardly knight with no excuse whatever,
For I will go to the Green Chapel, to get what Fate sends,
And have whatever words I wish with that worthy,
Whether weal or woe is what Fate
   Demands.

Fierce though that fellow be,
Clutching his club where he stands,*
Our Lord can certainly see
That his own are in safe hands.'

86

'By Mary!' said the other man, 'If you mean what you say,
You are determined to take all your trouble on yourself.
If you wish to lose your life, I'll no longer hinder you.
Here's your lance for your hand, your helmet for your head.
Ride down this rough track round yonder cliff
Till you arrive in a rugged ravine at the bottom,
Then look about on the flat, on your left hand,
And you will view there in the vale that very chapel,
And the grim gallant who guards it always.
Now, noble Gawain, good-bye in God's name.
For all the gold on God's earth I would not go with you,
Nor foot it an inch further through this forest as your fellow.'
Whereupon he wrenched at his reins, that rider in the woods,
Hit the horse with his heels as hard as he could,
Sent him leaping along, and left the knight there
        Alone.
    'By God!' said Gawain, 'I swear
    I will not weep or groan:
    Being given to God's good care,
    My trust in Him shall be shown.'

87

THEN he gave the spur to Gringolet and galloped down the path,
Thrust through a thicket there by a bank,
And rode down the rough slope right into the ravine.*
Then he searched about, but it seemed savage and wild,
And no sign did he see of any sort of building;
But on both sides banks, beetling and steep,
And great crooked crags, cruelly jagged;
The bristling barbs of rock seemed to brush the sky.
Then he held in his horse, halted there,
Scanned on every side in search of the chapel.
He saw no such thing anywhere, which seemed remarkable,
Save, hard by in the open, a hillock of sorts,
A smooth-surfaced barrow on a slope beside a stream
Which flowed forth fast there in its course,
Foaming and frothing as if feverishly boiling.
The knight, urging his horse, pressed onwards to the mound,
Dismounted manfully and made fast to a lime-tree
The reins, hooking them round a rough branch;
Then he went to the barrow, which he walked round, inspecting,
Wondering what in the world it might be.
It had a hole in each end and on either side,*
And was overgrown with grass in great patches.
All hollow it was within, only an old cavern
Or the crevice of an ancient crag: he could not explain it
      Aright.
    'O God, is the Chapel Green
    This mound?' said the noble knight.
    'At such might Satan be seen
    Saying matins at midnight.'

88

'Now certainly the place is deserted,' said Gawain,
'It is a hideous oratory, all overgrown,
And well graced for the gallant garbed in green
To deal out his devotions in the Devil's fashion.
Now I feel in my five wits, it is the Fiend himself
That has tricked me into this tryst, to destroy me here.
This is a chapel of mischance – checkmate to it!
It is the most evil holy place I ever entered.'
With his high helmet on his head, and holding his lance,
He roamed up to the roof of that rough dwelling.
Then from that height he heard, from a hard rock
On the bank beyond the brook, a barbarous noise.
What! It clattered amid the cliffs fit to cleave them apart,*
As if a great scythe were being ground on a grindstone there.
What! It whirred and it whetted like water in a mill.
What! It made a rushing, ringing din, rueful to hear.
'By God!' then said Gawain, 'that is going on,
I suppose, as a salute to myself, to greet me
           Hard by.
      God's will be warranted:
      "Alas!" is a craven cry.
      No din shall make me dread
      Although today I die.'

89

THEN the courteous knight called out clamorously,
'Who holds sway here and has an assignation with me?
For the good knight Gawain is on the ground here.

If anyone there wants anything, wend your way hither fast,
And further your needs either now, or not at all.'
'Bide there!' said one on the bank above his head,
'And you shall swiftly receive what I once swore to give you.'
Yet for a time he continued his tumult of scraping,
Turning away as he whetted, before he would descend.
Then he thrust himself round a thick crag through a hole,
Whirling round a wedge of rock with a frightful weapon,
A Danish axe duly honed for dealing the blow,★
With a broad biting edge, bow-bent along the handle,
Ground on a grindstone, a great four-foot blade –
No less, by that love-lace gleaming so brightly!★
And the gallant in green was garbed as at first,
His looks and limbs the same, his locks and beard;
Save that steadily on his feet he strode on the ground,
Setting the handle to the stony earth and stalking beside it.
He would not wade through the water when he came to it,
But vaulted over on his axe, then with huge strides
Advanced violently and fiercely along the field's width

      On the snow.
   Sir Gawain went to greet
   The knight, not bowing low.
   The man said, 'Sir so sweet,
   You honour the trysts you owe.'

90

'GAWAIN,' said the green knight, 'may God guard you!
You are welcome to my dwelling, I warrant you,
And you have timed your travel here as a true man ought.
You know plainly the pact we pledged between us:

This time a twelvemonth ago you took your portion,
And now at this New Year I should nimbly requite you.
And we are on our own here in this valley
With no seconds to sunder us, spar as we will.
Take your helmet off your head, and have your payment here.
And offer no more argument or action than I did
When you whipped off my head with one stroke.'
'No,' said Gawain, 'by God who gave me a soul,
The grievous gash to come I grudge you not at all;
Strike but the one stroke and I shall stand still
And offer you no hindrance; you may act freely,
   I swear.'
  Head bent, Sir Gawain bowed,
  And showed the bright flesh bare.
  He behaved as if uncowed,
  Being loth to display his care.

91

THEN the gallant in green quickly got ready,*
Heaved his horrid weapon on high to hit Gawain,
With all the brute force in his body bearing it aloft,
Swinging savagely enough to strike him dead.
Had it driven down as direly as he aimed,
The daring dauntless man would have died from the blow.
But Gawain glanced up at the grim axe beside him
As it came shooting through the shivering air to shatter him,
And his shoulders shrank slightly from the sharp edge.
The other suddenly stayed the descending axe,
And then reproved the prince with many proud words:
'You are not Gawain,' said the gallant, 'whose greatness is such

That by hill or hollow no army ever frightened him;
For now you flinch for fear before you feel harm.
I never did know that knight to be a coward.
I neither flinched nor fled when you let fly your blow,
Nor offered any quibble in the house of King Arthur.
My head flew to my feet, but flee I did not.
Yet you quail cravenly though unscathed so far.
So I am bound to be called the better man
       Therefore.'
   Said Gawain, 'Not again
   Shall I flinch as I did before;
   But if my head pitch to the plain,
   It's off for evermore.

92

'But be brisk, man, by your faith, and bring me to the point;*
Deal me my destiny and do it out of hand,
For I shall stand your stroke, not starting at all
Till your axe has hit me. Here is my oath on it.'
'Have at you then!' said the other, heaving up his axe,
Behaving as angrily as if he were mad.
He menaced him mightily, but made no contact,
Smartly withholding his hand without hurting him.
Gawain waited unswerving, with not a wavering limb,
But stood still as a stone or the stump of a tree
Gripping the rocky ground with a hundred grappling roots.
Then again the green knight began to gird:
'So now you have a whole heart I must hit you.
May the high knighthood which Arthur conferred
Preserve you and save your neck, if so it avail you!'

Then said Gawain, storming with sudden rage,
'Thrash on, you thrustful fellow, you threaten too much.
It seems your spirit is struck with self-dread.'
'Forsooth,' the other said, 'You speak so fiercely
I will no longer lengthen matters by delaying your business,
      I vow.'
    He stood astride to smite,
    Lips pouting, puckered brow.
    No wonder he lacked delight
    Who expected no help now.

93

UP went the axe at once and hurtled down straight
At the naked neck with its knife-like edge.
Though it swung down savagely, slight was the wound,
A mere snick on the side, so that the skin was broken.
Through the fair fat to the flesh fell the blade,
And over his shoulders the shimmering blood shot to the ground.
When Sir Gawain saw his gore glinting on the snow,
He leapt feet close together a spear's length away,*
Hurriedly heaved his helmet on to his head,
And shrugging his shoulders, shot his shield to the front,
Swung out his bright sword and said fiercely,
(For never had the knight since being nursed by his mother
Been so buoyantly happy, so blithe in this world)
'Cease your blows, sir, strike me no more.
I have sustained a stroke here unresistingly,
And if you offer any more I shall earnestly reply.
Resisting, rest assured, with the most rancorous
    Despite.

The single stroke is wrought
To which we pledged our plight
In high King Arthur's court:
Enough now, therefore, knight!'

94

THE bold man stood back and bent over his axe,
Putting the haft to earth, and leaning on the head.
He gazed at Sir Gawain on the ground before him,
Considering the spirited and stout way he stood,
Audacious in arms; his heart warmed to him.*
Then he gave utterance gladly in his great voice,
With resounding speech saying to the knight,
'Bold man, do not be so bloodily resolute.
No one here has offered you evil discourteously,
Contrary to the covenant made at the King's court.
I promised a stroke, which you received: consider yourself paid.
I cancel all other obligations of whatever kind.
If I had been more active, perhaps I could
Have made you suffer by striking a savager stroke.
First in foolery I made a feint at striking,
Not rending you with a riving cut – and right I was,
On account of the first night's covenant we accorded;
For you truthfully kept your trust in troth with me,
Giving me your gains, as a good man should.
The further feinted blow was for the following day,
When you kissed my comely wife, and the kisses came to me:
For those two things, harmlessly I thrust twice at you
        Feinted blows.

Truth for truth's the word;
No need for dread, God knows.
From your failure at the third
The tap you took arose.

95

'FOR that braided belt you wear belongs to me.
I am well aware that my own wife gave it you.
Your conduct and your kissings are completely known to me,
And the wooing by my wife – my work set it on.
I instructed her to try you, and you truly seem
To be the most perfect paladin ever to pace the earth.
As the pearl to the white pea in precious worth,
So in good faith is Gawain to other gay knights.
But here your faith failed you, you flagged somewhat, sir,
Yet it was not for a well-wrought thing, nor for wooing either,
But for love of your life, which is less blameworthy.'*
The other strong man stood considering this a while,
So filled with fury that his flesh trembled,*
And the blood from his breast burst forth in his face
As he shrank for shame at what the chevalier spoke of.
The first words the fair knight could frame were:
'Curses on both cowardice and covetousness!
Their vice and villainy are virtue's undoing.'
Then he took the knot, with a twist twitched it loose,
And fiercely flung the fair girdle to the knight.
'Lo! There is the false thing, foul fortune befall it!
I was craven about our encounter, and cowardice taught me
To accord with covetousness and corrupt my nature
And the liberality and loyalty belonging to chivalry.

Now I am faulty and false and found fearful always.
In the train of treachery and untruth go woe
       And shame.
    I acknowledge, knight, how ill
    I behaved, and take the blame.
    Award what penance you will:
    Henceforth I'll shun ill-fame.'

96

THEN the other lord laughed and politely said,
'In my view you have made amends for your misdemeanour;
You have confessed your faults fully with fair acknowledgement,
And plainly done penance at the point of my axe.
You are absolved of your sin and as stainless now
As if you had never fallen in fault since first you were born.
As for the gold-hemmed girdle, I give it you, sir,
Seeing it is as green as my gown. Sir Gawain, you may
Think about this trial when you throng in company
With paragons of princes, for it is a perfect token,
At knightly gatherings, of the great adventure at the Green Chapel.
You shall come back to my castle this cold New Year,
And we shall revel away the rest of this rich feast;
       Let us go.'
    Thus urging him, the lord
    Said, 'You and my wife, I know
    We shall bring to clear accord,
    Though she was your fierce foe.'

97

'No, forsooth,' said the knight, seizing his helmet,
And doffing it with dignity as he delivered this thanks,
'My stay has sufficed me. Still, luck go with you!

May He who bestows all good, honour you with it!
And commend me to the courteous lady, your comely wife;
Indeed, my due regards to both dear ladies,
Who with their wanton wiles have thus waylaid their knight.
But it is no marvel for a foolish man to be maddened thus★
And saddled with sorrow by the sleights of women.
For here on earth was Adam taken in by one,
And Solomon by many such, and Samson likewise;
Delilah dealt him his doom; and David, later still,
Was blinded by Bathsheba, and badly suffered for it.
Since these were troubled by their tricks, it would be true joy
To love them but not believe them, if a lord could,
For these were the finest of former times, most favoured by fortune
Of all under the heavenly kingdom whose hearts were
            Abused;
        These four all fell to schemes
        Of women whom they used.
        If I am snared, it seems
        I ought to be excused.

98

'But your girdle,' said Gawain, 'God requite you for it!
Not for the glorious gold shall I gladly wear it,
Nor for the stuff nor the silk nor the swaying pendants,
Nor for its worth, fine workmanship or wonderful honour;

But as a sign of my sin I shall see it often,
Remembering with remorse, when I am mounted in glory,
The fault and faintheartedness of the perverse flesh,
How it tends to attract tarnishing sin.
So when pride shall prick me for my prowess in arms,
One look at this love-lace will make lowly my heart.
But one demand I make of you, may it not incommode you:
Since you are master of the demesne I have remained in a while,
Make known, by your knighthood – and now may He above,
Who sits on high and holds up heaven, requite you! –
How you pronounce your true name; and no more requests.'
'Truly,' the other told him, 'I shall tell you my title.
Bertilak of the High Desert I am called here in this land.*
Through the might of Morgan the Fay, who remains in my house,*
Through the wiles of her witchcraft, a lore well learned –
Many of the magical arts of Merlin she acquired,*
For she lavished fervent love long ago
On that susceptible sage: certainly your knights know
        Of their fame.
    So "Morgan the Goddess"
    She accordingly became;
    The proudest she can oppress
    And to her purpose tame –

99

'SHE sent me forth in this form to your famous hall
To put to the proof the great pride of the house,
The reputation for high renown of the Round Table;
She bewitched me in this weird way to bewilder your wits,
And to grieve Guinevere and goad her to death

With ghastly fear of that ghost's ghoulish speaking
With his head in his hand before the high table.
That is the aged beldame who is at home:
She is indeed your own aunt, Arthur's half-sister,
Daughter of the Duchess of Tintagel who in due course,
By Uther, was mother of Arthur, who now holds sway.
Therefore I beg you, bold sir, come back to your aunt,
Make merry in my house, for my men love you,
And by my faith, brave sir, I bear you as much good will
As I grant any man under God, for your great honesty.'
But Gawain firmly refused with a final negative.
They clasped and kissed, commending each other
To the Prince of Paradise, and parted on the cold ground
                    Right there.
          Gawain on steed serene
          Spurred to court with courage fair,
          And the gallant garbed in green
          To wherever he would elsewhere.*

                         100

N o w Gawain goes riding on Gringolet
In lonely lands, his life saved by grace.
Often he stayed at a house, and often in the open,
And often overcame hazards in the valleys,
Which at this time I do not intend to tell you about.
The hurt he had had in his neck was healed,
And the glittering girdle that girt him round
Obliquely, like a baldric, was bound by his side
And laced under the left arm with a lasting knot,*
In token that he was taken in a tarnishing sin;

And so he came to court, quite unscathed.
When the great became aware of Gawain's arrival
There was general jubilation at the joyful news.
The King kissed the knight, and the Queen likewise,
And so did many a staunch noble who sought to salute him.
They all asked him about his expedition,
And he truthfully told them of his tribulations –
What chanced at the chapel, the good cheer of the knight,
The lady's love-making, and lastly, the girdle.
He displayed the scar of the snick on his neck
Where the bold man's blow had hit, his bad faith to

      Proclaim;
  He groaned at his disgrace,
  Unfolding his ill-fame,
  And blood suffused his face
  When he showed his mark of shame.

101

'Look, my lord,' said Gawain, the lace in his hand.
'This belt confirms the blame I bear on my neck,
My bane and debasement, the burden I bear
For being caught by cowardice and covetousness.
This is the figure of the faithlessness found in me,
Which I must needs wear while I live.
For man can conceal sin but not dissever from it,
So when it is once fixed, it will never be worked loose.'
First the King, then all the court, comforted the knight,
And all the lords and ladies belonging to the Table
Laughed at it loudly, and concluded amiably
That each brave man of the brotherhood should bear a baldric,*

A band, obliquely about him, of bright green,
Of the same hue as Sir Gawain's and for his sake wear it.
So it ranked as renown to the Round Table,
And an everlasting honour to him who had it,
As is rendered in Romance's rarest book.
Thus in the days of Arthur this exploit was achieved,
To which the books of Brutus bear witness;
After the bold baron, Brutus, came here,
The siege and the assault being ceased at Troy
   Before.
  Such exploits, I'll be sworn,
  Have happened here of yore.
  Now Christ with his crown of thorn
  Bring us his bliss evermore! AMEN

HONY SOYT QUI MAL PENCE

The Common Enemy of Man

THE Green Knight is such an extraordinary artistic creation that the reader is tempted to let him steal the show as the old stage devils used to, and go well beyond giving him his due as the formal antagonist in the poem. Even a superficial summary of his manifestations which leaves out most of his complexities will show how hard it is to achieve a unified focus on him. Thus, on his first appearance he is described successively as a terrifying giant (ll. 137–40), a handsome and well-built knight (ll. 141–6), a weirdly green – and hence, implicitly supernatural – person (ll. 147–50), as excessively hairy (ll. 180–86) like that common creature of popular mythology, the wild man of the woods, and as a mocking enchanter (ll. 309–15). And on his last appearance, besides these, he appears as a warm and sympathetic human being (ll. 2333–6), an omniscient confessor who judges with accuracy and compassion, and above all with authority (ll. 2338–99), and finally as a human, subtly diminished by the termination of his supernatural function (ll. 2400–70).

The suggestions of these first and last manifestations are richly filled out and diversified in the second and third fits by the character-ization and activity of Sir Bertilak, the Green Knight's other self. In this essay I shall try, by tracing through the poem the operation of the mechanism that tests Sir Gawain, to focus on the nature of the Green Knight and of the supernatural in the poem generally; to examine some of the ambiguities without resolving all of them; and, by doing these things, to prepare for an approach to the whole meaning of the poem through an examination of the role of the hero.

I call the Green Knight 'the common enemy of man' – Macbeth's periphrasis for the Devil. The Hebrew word 'Satan' in fact means 'adversary' and there is no doubt that the Green Knight is Sir Gawain's adversary. But what sort of enemy? On the whole he seems friendly to Gawain, and cannot be classified as a conventional devil of Christian myth; that is, a damned soul hungering for relief from torment, which he deludedly imagines he can achieve by luring other souls to damnation. The Green Knight is more like the jovial demon of old popular tradition, and also, it seems to me, resembles the kind of devil who tempts within the system and on behalf of God, like Satan in the Book of Job; he knows what good and evil are. But his first appearance is absolutely unequivocal: everything, from Arthur's initial invocation of a 'marvel', right through the detail of the description of the Green Knight, leads straight to the conclusion of the court that he is a 'phantom from Fairyland' (l. 240). And the structure of events in the poem requires that he remain that, however benevolent he may appear to be from time to time.

But he is no stock phantom derived from popular superstition: rather he is a composite figure who, though alien and hostile to Arthur's court, can probe with certainty its most cherished and subtle predilections. Thus, his first request to be granted 'good sport' (ll. 256–74) is couched in as courteous terms and tone (except for his familiarity in using the second person singular to King Arthur) as the strictest chivalric code could demand. His next speech is quite different. Here (ll. 279–300) is the typical boasting challenge of the feudal world, stripped of courtesy but justly specific in procedural detail. But it produces only awe-struck silence, and appropriately enough, since chivalrous knights should take up challenges at once, the Green Knight turns churl, rolling his furious red eyes before mocking the cowardice of Arthur's court (ll. 303–15). His role as just moral critic is thus established virtually at the start, yet the terror of his aspect, his violence of speech and action remain. Actual or implied imperatives, and sudden strong movements, equally express this phantom's essence, and the fury and finality of everything he says and does are heightened by a menacing and humorous irony, such as that of his last speech before his head is struck off (ll. 404–12). After he has gone, the courteously false laughter of Arthur and Gawain, and Arthur's much-needed words of comfort to Guinevere (ll. 462–75), underline the horror of the experience the Green Knight has given the court.

So far, the modern reader will have needed little arcane knowledge of medieval matters to understand broadly what is going on. But the next significant step does take him into a slightly specialized world which the medieval listener or reader would have been expected to know. After Gawain's departure from civilized Camelot and his journey through an obviously hostile winter landscape, he arrives at what will turn out to be the seat of his enemy. It is in a country recognizably like that of the approach to the Other World as described in Celtic folklore. The unpleasant wasteland shades off into a valley of trees under a mountain, and the castle, when it suddenly appears, lies in a pleasant enclosure behind a water barrier. Of the trees mentioned in lines 742–4, Mother Angela Carson (Bibliography 15, p. 11) writes:

> Each of these trees has its peculiar significance: hawthorn is often thought to be the haunt of fairies; the roots of the oak supposedly reach to the Other World; and hazel, sometimes connected with a preternatural wisdom, is also considered a charm against enchantment.

She attaches great importance to the sudden appearance of the castle, which she considers could have aroused the reader's suspicion, and remarks that the passing of the water barrier is a sign that the Other World has been reached.

But the poet's evocation of his own distinctive other world is deliberately ambiguous. Gawain perceives the castle as the direct result of a Christian prayer that he may do proper service to God on the following day, Christmas Day; and if that fact is presented by the poet as a deliberate false trail, then everything good about the castle is also false – its welcoming hospitality, its courteous manners, the priests who conduct its ceremonies of worship. That would make every person in the castle a pawn in a supernatural conspiracy against Gawain, and it would be shocking decorum for the poet to write of such people, when Gawain takes leave of them the night before setting off for the Green Chapel (ll. 1987–8):

> And every soul was as sad to say farewell
> As if they had always had the hero in their house.

It is not a tenable thesis although, when at the Green Chapel the Green Knight declares himself to have been Gawain's host at the castle, the reader, having been given the key to the poem's meaning, at once goes back over all the events since Gawain's arrival at the castle and tries to find in them evidence of supernatural deception. He will certainly find some, but it will be conclusive in only one respect: it will establish the duality of the powers against which Gawain finds himself contending. And this is especially true of Morgan and the host's wife.

These ladies are not named while they are with Gawain: it is only at the Green Chapel that the identity of the elder is given. Nevertheless, the poet provides evidence both direct and circumstantial that they are enchantresses. The beauty of the Lady, which *seemed* to Gawain to excel that of Guinevere (ll. 943–5), is suspicious, since Arthur's queen was known to be the most beautiful woman on earth. And the ugliness of the old lady would amount to fairly strong evidence of a past in which she practised witchcraft, or lechery, or both. Yet these two ladies constantly display courtesy – a term which includes noble manners, Christian belief and fine feelings.

How, then, to explain the Lady's direct offer of her body to Gawain (l. 1237)? In Romance, there are two sorts of woman who declare their desire openly. One is the lady who vows *service* to a knight with whom she has fallen in love, either because he appears marvellously attractive or because he has done her some special favour such as saving her life or her chastity; and she may be declaring an attitude rather than offering her body, though the latter offer might be implicit. The second kind of woman, who is an enchantress, wants to enslave the knight or deflect him from a quest in which loss of his chastity would be fatal to success, and so appeals directly to his lust. The Lady is fundamentally the latter type, and camouflages the fact by assuming the attitude and language of the former. Her purpose is never in doubt, and is in fact specifically emphasized by the poet in line 1734 as he proceeds to describe the especially seductive décolletage she assumes for her last attempt on Gawain's chastity.

The Lady's technique is basically similar to that of Morgan and her familiars in other romances, whose victims become enslaved to their magic the moment they fornicate with them. It is only when her blunt offer fails on the first occasion that she falls back on the refined technique of 'love-talk'; only when her love-talk fails to compromise Gawain in the slightest that she falls back on a temptation which lures him to a minor sin which has almost nothing to do with love – telling a lie to the host in breach of a promise, in order to safeguard his life. But here, as elsewhere, the poet builds in a masterly ambiguity, because a green girdle sensually unfastened from a lady's waist and securely lapped about a man's certainly seems like a love-token, and would be taken as such by anyone who noticed it.

So I read both ladies as Morgans: their composite qualities give us what we need to make sense of the crucial constructive device in the poem – that element which securely binds the Temptation and the Exchange of Winnings themes to the theme of the Beheading Game. They are ambiguously recognizable as Morgans from their first appearance and, as Morgans, their moral ambiguity is not to be read simply as diabolical camouflage for irremediable evil. Both the old lady and the hostess keep something of their prototype's benevolence – that healing quality in Morgan which makes the dying Arthur sail with her to Avalon – with their heartfelt solicitude at his departure for the Green Chapel (ll. 1982–3), and the promise, conveyed by Sir Bertilak (ll. 2403–6 and ll. 2467–70), of renewed communion and solicitude, the contest being behind them.

All the same, to the reader the main reality of the Lady lies in her threat to Gawain's chastity and courtesy, a respect in which she conforms to a pattern found in the Anglo-Norman *Yder* (discussed by Larry D. Benson, Bibliography 4, p. 38) and in folk tales of other cultures. She is the wife of the host, who is deliberately offered to the guest: if the guest falls to her wiles, he becomes a prey of the husband.

In *Yder*, the hero has to withstand the advances of Ivenant's queen in order to be granted arms by King Ivenant; he kicks her in the belly, and even when he has successfully repulsed her, he will bid farewell to her only through a shut door. In *Sir Gawain and the Green Knight*, the host pairs our hero-guest with his wife at the Christmas Day feast (ll. 1003-4), arranges for her to keep company with him during the first hunt (ll. 1097-9), and again pairs her with him at the supper after the boar-hunt (l. 1657). When the revelations are made at the Green Chapel, the full situation, with its fascinating vistas of collusion between host and hostess, progress reports and planning, becomes clear. It is the opposite of climactic suspense that we are offered; a contemplative retrospect, which throws light ever more diversely-hued and ambiguous on the figure of the Antagonist.

To that question posed earlier – 'What sort of enemy?' – the main response so far has been to emphasize his duality and describe the mechanism of which he is the instrument. It is now time to consider him in more detail, taking up no more than the text suggests, and starting with his first appearance.

When all the variegated detail summarized at the beginning of this essay has been absorbed, for the people in the poem, the nobles and servants in King Arthur's court, one essential stands out. Their visitor is green, and that means that he is dead, an evil revenant intent on finding a victim in the court and killing him by magic trickery (ll. 240, 680-81). But for the reader, other qualities are present. Green is also the colour of spring and vegetation, and, when linked with gold, is symbolic of youth. Vigorous and peremptory the Green Knight certainly is, but little ought to be built on the use of similes drawn from nature to describe his greenness (grass in l. 235) or his hairiness (bush in l. 181), simply because these similes are about as conventional as similes can be. His energy and humour seem to me incredibly earthy and mature, and altogether lacking in the tremulous and spring-like quality associated with youth. It is Gawain, not the Green Knight, who is eventually compared with a tree (ll. 2293-4, when he is awaiting the axe-stroke), and is implicitly presented as spring personified (ll. 866–8), when freshly dressed after his arrival at the northern castle.

Yet the Green Knight's combination of greenness, hairiness, energy, earthiness and mainly rough, imperative speech incline us irrevocably to think of two common medieval types, one an outcast and the other a rural deity. The wild man of the woods, the 'wodwose', was often an outlaw who had taken to the woods and there developed sub-human habits and the fierce unpredictable behaviour of a wild beast. The green man, on the other hand, was a personification of spring, a mythological supernatural being who persists to this day in English folk dance and in the name of many pubs. Larry D. Benson (Bibliography 4, p. 75) writes:

> In popular belief the two figures (i.e. the wild and the green man) are closely linked, and in folk ritual they are interchange-able . . . However, in literary works the two figures are quite distinct. A close association with nature is the only quality they share, and even this reveals a contrast.

The contrast to which Benson refers is that between wild winter and green summer. I would add that green and wild man share an op-position to the formal state of things: the green man, with his natural fertility and spring incitement to concupiscence, is opposed to Christ-ianity, and the wild man, with his churlish crudity and criminality, is opposed to the noble feudal order. J. A. Burrow (Bibliography 14, p. 47) quotes a medieval tag used in the education of noble children:

> All vertus be closyde in curtasy
> And alle vyces in vilony.

In fact, as Benson remarks (Bibliography 4, p. 21) referring to the pattern of earlier beheading tales, 'The challenger seemed just as clearly to fit this scheme, for his ugliness, hairiness, gigantic size, and axe are the contemporary marks of the literary *vilain*, the traditional op-ponent of the Romance knight.'

The axe no doubt had the significance Benson attaches to it because it was the characteristic weapon of the heathen Norse invaders, turbulent enemies of the Christian estate in England. The poet does not even hint at a suggestion made by some critics, that it is an attribute (and anthropologists might wish to call it a phallic attribute) of a sun-god. But I prefer to think of the Green Knight's axe in parallel with other frames of reference, along the theological lines so constantly favoured by this poet, and to see it functioning as a truth-bringer; which is how John the Baptist saw the coming of Christ:

> And now also the axe is laid unto the root of the trees . . . he that cometh after me is mightier than I . . . he will thoroughly purge his floor . . . (Authorized Version, Matthew 3, 10–12)

Truth-bringing is certainly the main achievement of the Green Knight, however diverse his activities and antecedents; and it surprises me that no critic has picked up one very important medieval theological reference to green as the colour of truth. This is in the first great English morality play, *The Castle of Perseverance*, which was written in the north-eastern Midlands at about the end of the fourteenth century – that is, within a few years of this poem. The instruction in it for the clothing of the Four Daughters of God who eventually take charge of the soul of Mankind reads (I modernize the spelling):

> The iiii daughters shall be clad in mantles, Mercy in white, Righteousness in red altogether, Truth in sad green, and Peace all in black . . . (The Macro Plays, ed. Mark Eccles, EETS, OUP, 1969, p. 1)

So 'sad green' – and 'sad' then meant sober and settled – was a colour with a symbolic value which the author expected to be understood; not surprisingly, evergreen, which is a *sad* green, is the colour assigned to ever-living and eternal truth (*Veritas Dei manet in aeternum* – the truth of God remains in eternity). And since the evidence of the staging arrangements, and the impossibility of presenting the play with fewer than twenty-one actors, show beyond reasonable doubt that each presentation was a grand public affair, the author of *The Castle* expected this symbolism to be understood by a mass audience. The Green Knight, both before having his head cut off and after nicking Gawain's neck, prodigally refers to truth. All this is not to say that medieval colour symbolism was an exact science, or that green did not ever stand for qualities remote from Truth.

These qualities of wild man, green man, villein, giant, demon, symbolic truth-bringer, which the Green Knight displays at first are subtly metamorphosed when his alter ego, the host of the northern castle, appears. The size and the power are there again, but instead of green, there is a ruddy quality about the man. His beard is luxuriant and 'beaver-hued'. The beaver's coat, the latent red glow of which is brought out when the light catches it and may remind one of fire or the sun, seems to have fascinated people in the Middle Ages, and to have become, like ruddy-brown hair in men, symbolic of vigorous life. Such an intent worker and builder, that animal, transforming its habitat all the time – and of course it was common in England in those days. The strength and ruddiness of the host are emphasized at once with a fire image – 'His face was fierce as fire'. But it is not destructive fire, and his courtesy and good manners are repeatedly stressed. It is not until he begins to heap special hospitality on his guest that we become aware of a kind of irresistible superabundance of spirit in him, which is at once incongruous within the concept of courtesy because it is immoderate, and so headlong and precipitate that we are reminded of the visitant of the first fit:

> Lightning-like he seemed
> And swift to strike and stun.

As Cecily Clark (Bibliography 16, p. 365) rather nicely puts it:

> There are other ways for inviting a guest to prolong his stay
> (and a subtle man such as Gawain would have found them) than

seizing his lapel and beating him into submission with imperatives and peremptory *shall's* while at the same time establishing a detailed and fixed programme for the rest of his visit.

She might have added that almost every hospitable suggestion, or plan for a wager, of the host in the second fit is accompanied by a huge gust of laughter. Whereas the tone of the first fit is mainly tragic, that of the second and third fits is comic: a difference largely determined by the two personae of the Antagonist, who is properly a menacing though jovial demon for the Beheading Game, and an uproarious knight for the Exchange of Winnings. In the latter plot, the idea that sexual gains can be traded for concrete things like animal hunt trophies takes the whole tone dangerously near to that of fabliau (the short comic verse tale of anything but noble life, in which satire and bawdry were common).

Leaving aside that aspect of the host manifested in the hunting episodes (see Introduction pp. 16–18), I turn to the events of the last fit. It is the dead of winter, the season in which all the events of the poem happen. The place to which the guide brings Gawain is a wilderness, and the Green Chapel is described by the guide and recognized by Gawain as the haunt of an evil enchanter. J. A. Burrow (Bibliography 14, p. 119) finds it odd that 'the Green Knight is presented as an ancient and well-known local hazard – when nearly everything else in the poem (notably Bertilak's own explanations at the end) suggests that he is simply a device, a "wonder", contrived by Morgan le [*sic*] Fay on this one occasion to trouble Guinevere and the Round Table.' But the guide, surely, is part of the supernatural mechanism, neither good nor evil, but functioning as a tester and tempter, just like the host and the hostess. Unless the chapel-haunting monster is a 'well-known local hazard', Gawain might wonder how his new friends at the castle could come to direct him: and accordingly the reader's apprehension of the supernatural power faced by the hero, which needs to be constant from the start until the unravelling of the dénouement, might be destroyed.

At the Green Chapel, everything the Green Knight does, until the moment when he withholds his third stroke, is made as terrifying as possible, so that Gawain's keeping to the letter of his promise made a year before is especially meritorious. The placing and appearance of the barrow are hellish and, as on his first appearance, the arrival of the Green Knight is heralded by noise. This time it is the sharpening of an axe on a bank above Gawain's head, and the description of the axe-wielder approaching Gawain (ll. 2217-34) is for me the most terrifying thing in the poem, building as it does on the earlier description of the headless green man holding the talking head in his hand. Even the Green Knight's deplorable quibble about his own bravery and Gawain's cowardice (ll. 2270-79) is in the worst tradition of misleading tempters, and could reasonably be expected to lead to some peculiarly diabolical act of cruelty and dread. But once the terror is over, and judgement begins, a remarkable change comes over the Green Knight. In the story structure, he behaves as his forebears did in earlier Beheading Game stories, complimenting his adversary on his bravery and good faith in keeping the appointment; and it is accordingly possible to undervalue his behaviour at this stage, since superficially it appears satisfyingly to echo that of the comparable figure in the analogues.

A close look at the Green Knight's speech (ll. 2338-68) as he leans nonchalantly on his axe, his heart warming to his former adversary, shows how the poet has transcended his models and significantly changed the emphasis. Throughout the speech there is a refined moral attitude which is stated with accuracy and delight against a background of just such frightening ambiguities as underlie the debate in the book of Job. After his ringing denial that he has offered Gawain any evil, he says (ll. 2343-4):

> If I had been more active, perhaps I could
> Have made you suffer by striking a savager stroke.

The poet's French word 'deliver' (active, nimble, quick) was generally used in a concrete rather than abstract sense; so I take the Green Knight to be making a deprecatory joke about his own physical capacity. But he follows that with the enigmatic 'perhaps', which prompts the thought that, as the supernatural agent of an essentially moral force, 'perhaps' he could not have struck off Gawain's head even if he had tried, Gawain's fault not meriting such a punishment as beheading. The fault, which I shall discuss in the next essay, derives from the second strand of the plot, that concerned with the Temptation and the Exchange of Winnings; in the analogues of the Beheading Game element, there is no fault. So it is from the precise point of interaction between the two plots that the final significance of the Antagonist emerges: he is a judge possessing something like divine authority, who pronounces unerringly from a moral standpoint determined by the complementary ideals of chivalry and Christianity.

He pinpoints Gawain's fault, confesses him in his shame and guilt, defines his penance and declares that he is absolved. It is the highest and least enigmatic manifestation of this many-sided character.

After that, in what has been described as a perfunctory explanation of his function, the Green Knight as a character evolves still further in a series of enigmatic, and therefore more interesting, reverberations all of which echo aspects of that multiform self deriving in part from the analogues and in part from the original creation of the poet. As a temporary enchanter resuming human face after discarding his super-natural mask, he wants and apparently needs both to bask in the light of a human virtue which he cannot himself have, and to atone for his tempting by expressing friendship and admiration (ll. 2399–2406). As the Tempter of the analogues, he explains his identity and function (ll. 2444–66); and in the light of what is apparently a statement of final reconciliation, which includes an implicit promise that all hostility, even from Morgan, is over, he again presses his human invitation. In that invitation, and in Gawain's 'final negative', we understand the isolation from humanity of the shape-shifter, his con-finement in a diabolical world where the best human values can be appreciated and envied but not shared. And we also understand the necessary separation of good from evil: Gawain's experience is behind him, though the lesson he has learnt from it, symbolized by the green girdle, will be with him for ever. The last enigma of the Green Knight is the manner of his departure. If the literal sense of the foregoing argument has been reflected in the Green Knight's appearance, from the moment when he leaned upon his axe, with his heart warming towards Gawain, he would have started to lose his greenness and frightfulness, and would have gradually turned into the ruddy and magnificent Sir Bertilak, a Bertilak who developed 'angel-having' (a term the poet uses to describe the virtually holy child-apparition in *Pearl*) before stumbling, at the last, into the posture of a nostalgic pleader.

According to the patterns set up in the analogues, the Tempter should either, in his reformed state, join the Round Table (as suggested by Albert B. Friedman, Bibliography 17, p. 270), or, as a defeated enchanter, really die. In either case, he loses his supernatural status. In the Green Knight's apparent relief that his task is over there is an echo of another idea sometimes found in Romance: the hero having succeeded 'in coming through in safety, they [i.e. the enchanters] rejoice with him for with his success comes their release' (G. L. Kittredge, Bibliography 18, p. 81). But the poet firmly leaves the Green Knight green, describes him sharing a Christian blessing, and dispatches him 'To wherever he would elsewhere', not even to gloomy self-commiseration in a castle no longer lit by the Christian chivalry of Gawain. By that single line, which expresses in terms conventional to the genre a sense of the continuing and unpredictable operation of the Faerie, the Green Knight keeps his mystery as a natural force. The last exit line of the Green Knight parallels the first (l. 460). The line of Spenser that I quoted in a note to l. 460 serves as a summary epigraph for him:

And *Natur's* selfe did vanish, whither no man wist.

Gawain's 'Eternal Jewel'

To entitle my two chief critical contributions to this book 'The Common Enemy of Man' and 'Gawain's "Eternal Jewel"' is to assert that the core of the poem's meaning is religious and ethical, and to remind the reader that Gawain, unlike Macbeth, did not give his 'eternal jewel to the common enemy of man'. But though the structure of the poem – its main events, their order, the way in which they are interpreted, and the upshot – supports this reading, the assertion must be made good in full knowledge and appreciation of what constitutes, in addition to the core, the essence of the whole poem. Among these 'essences' are heightened forms of traditional Romance elements: decoration, as of beautiful people, courts and castles, pageantry,

armour – beauties and graces both static and in motion; knightly action, as tourneying, dancing and singing, hunting; and love-talk, for the lords of Romance the highest court activity, just as fighting was the highest field occupation. Other essences derive from an older world: those suggestions of Celtic and still more primitive myth which underlie the characterization and activity of the Green Knight in particular, and the briefly mentioned adventures of Gawain on his northward journey; the typically northern background of harsh winter, which dominates the poem except for the short and beautiful account of the seasonal cycle at the beginning of the second fit – and even that takes the reader from winter to winter.

In this wonderful weave, which is richly drab with the constant dread of the main story, the comic strands glint brightly. This is partly because the antagonist is a jovial moral demon who enjoys his role and whose rhetorical method is ironic, and partly because the situation of Gawain's longest test, that of a man resisting a woman's advances, is fundamentally funny. But matters of comedy aside, our sympathy is with the hero, because he is a human, because he is the hero and because by entering his predicaments we can recognize our own. Gawain's battle to retain his self-respect as a virtuous and religious knight gives the poem its final and only discernible shape.

The first clue to the morality of the hero lies in his identity. By the fourteenth century, in Europe and southern England, the literary vogue of treating Arthurian material was in decline, and the values associated with its heyday were weakening just as chivalry itself, the code which dominated life and society until the social changes connected with the Renaissance began to bite into it, was also weakening. This historical process was reflected in changes in the literature; in which sphere the one change of concern to us is the development of Sir Gawain from the exemplar of chivalry – honourably susceptible to love and a great warrior loyal to his King – in early Arthurian literature to the equivocal figure of the later literature who is adept at seduction and finally treacherous. But the alliterative verse revival of the west and north-west of England drew its strength, in subject matter as in tone and poetic forms, from the earlier tradition. So our poem presents the Gawain to whom Chaucer makes his Squire refer – his Squire, a young man so dazzled by romantic subject matter that he inchoately pours out streams of different yarns together, fails to achieve any sort of unity, and is interrupted just when he has made a hiccoughy promise to continue with three of the subjects of his Tale. Our hero is

> Gawayn, with his olde curteisye.

This is the Gawain we first meet (l. 340), a knight of luminous chivalric purity asking if he may take over the challenge his feudal lord has accepted. The elaborate courtesy, the refined and evidently heartfelt humility, the hesitant conditionals, the address to the Queen as well as to the King, the appeal to sanctions of both courtly manners and the blood relationship, and the compliment and final reference to 'this full court': all are in due and perfect form, and the speech fixes the hero in a pattern which would be recognized at once, a pattern by which he would be judged throughout his subsequent adventures. 'The perfect knight is a lion on the field of battle, and a lamb in hall' (D. S. Brewer, Bibliography 5, p. 77).

'Courteous' in the old sense is what every member of the poet's audience would expect Gawain to be. But the poet shows himself above all interested in another quality, which could indeed be comprehended by various extended meanings of the word 'courtesy', though 'courtesy' is not the poet's term. His quality is *truth* – literal truth, good faith in dealing with others, good faith in dealing with oneself in relation to an accepted scheme of values. The concept enters the poem with the Tempter; the Green Knight and Gawain repeatedly invoke it as they go over their bargain (ll. 378–412). Throughout Gawain's trials, till the very end of the poem, truth in the sense of good faith remains the chief concern of the hero, though pursuit of it naturally involves him in the defence of other virtues, such as courtesy, generosity, loyalty, moderation, bravery and chastity. His last words in the poem (ll. 2505–12) refer to the girdle as 'the figure of the faithlessness found' in him: for the definition of the 'good faith' to which he aspired to hold, we must turn to that other 'figure', the sign of the Pentangle.

The point in the manuscript at which the poet introduces it (l. 619) is marked by a coloured initial, and the sign is described at once as one of holy origin betokening truth (l. 626). It is worth emphasizing the 'fiveness' of the multiple concept of 'truth': the five wits and five fingers make up the spiritual and physical human self which can practise virtue or vice; the five wounds of Christ and the five joys of the Virgin stand for heaven's grace and power in man's moral and spiritual life; and the 'pure five' virtues (see note to ll. 652–4) make up the 'truth' of which the whole pentangle, the parts of which harmoniously and inextricably merge with each other, is the emblem. This complex 'truth' has the special significance of being established as the knight's symbol and motto immediately before he sets out on his quest. It will therefore remain the central concern of the adventures and of the poem itself.

As if to emphasize this point, the poet at once ostentatiously neglects to describe his hero exercising the conventional knightly virtue – courage. Scores of battles with enemies natural and supernatural Sir Gawain had on his northward journey but, writes the poet, 'It would be too tedious to tell a tenth of them'. This is not so much to offer an ironic critique on the lurid excesses of the genre of Romance as to hurry over details the telling of which would pull his story design out of shape. His pious endurance, the quality in this time of peril which is relevant to the subject of the poem, is dwelt on instead (ll. 724–5); it will take him to the scene of his hardest trial.

The test of the encounters with the Lady is the main one because its outcome determines the result of the Beheading Game, and the hardest because Gawain does not know of any connection between his compact with the Green Knight and his compact with Lord of the Castle. This makes it an altogether loftier matter than any formal test could be, because it is his ordinary self in its day-to-day moral functioning without pressure from specific vows that is on trial. Of course what happens between Gawain and the Lady is related in all sorts of ways to the rest of his situation. It could not be otherwise to a whole man. For example, though it may be noted that the maintenance of chastity until a quest has been achieved is 'normal', it is not so stated in the poem; there is no special chastity at stake. Chastity is only a factor in the Exchange of Winnings game, not a first principle of the poem. On the other hand the principle of good faith is firmly attached to the girdle. This is a concrete gain which ought to be declared; and not to declare it is an 'untruth'.

What inducements to abandon 'truth' appear to Gawain in his day-to-day moral functioning in the castle of Bertilak? Donald R. Howard (Bibliography 13, p. 59) notes most helpfully that according to Catholic orthodoxy stemming from Augustine, three steps go to make up sin: suggestion, delectation and consent:

> Now suggestion was itself blameless unless somehow responded to: consent, on the other hand was rational intention and determination to sin. The ambiguous point at which temptation became sin was therefore centred in the notion of delectation. Was it sin to be 'delighted' with a suggestion if one did not give it full and rational consent? (p. 63)

Let us consider the element of suggestion first. Gawain finds that he is expected to teach his hosts the 'converse of courtly love' (l. 926), an expectation to which he could hardly object since 'love-talking' 'was not the prelude to seduction on Gawain's part, not indecent, but *very* delightful and *very* polite, and presumably about love, the favourite topic of medieval courtly conversation' (D. S. Brewer, Bibliography 5, p. 70). The initiative he shows in the castle chapel (l. 935) and his admiration of his hostess after the service must therefore be understood as courtly rather than sexual: a knight can only discourse of love with a beautiful woman. But in the whole of the poem there is no evidence that the poet accepts the orthodox courtly love teaching that 'One cannot be courteous unless one loves' (Marie de France: *Guigemar*, 59, quoted by D. S. Brewer, Bibliography 5, p. 77). I find therefore no suggestion to sin in the situation which Gawain accepts and partly determines on his arrival at the castle.

It is quite a different matter on the morning of the first hunt, when the Lady visits his bedchamber. Her offer of her body, and her inference that if Gawain is true to his reputation, he will accept it, is suggestion indeed. Gawain's response shows that on this occasion he is not suggestible at all, and that his courtesy and tact can preserve his 'truth' for him:

> To reject her advances bluntly would be to insult her. To accept them would be to betray his position as the Host's guest. If he can neither accept not reject them, to acknowledge them would be barbarous. The civilized way to handle such a problem is to pretend that it does not even exist. Gawain's tact is equal to the occasion ... Beneath the jesting dalliance, the gay banter and merry colloquy that Gawain and the Hostess carry on for three mornings in a row, there is always the sober substance of her adulterous intention and his determination to thwart it. (Morton Donner, Bibliography 19, p. 311)

His sole reproof, an implied one veiled as a compliment to her taste in selecting a mate, is his reference to her husband as a better man than himself (l. 1276). By making Gawain say such a thing, the poet is rejecting on behalf of the hero the glamorous and often adulterous *amour courtois* upon which the world of Romance literature fed, and placing himself beside serious literary moralists like the poet of the much earlier *The Owl and the Nightingale* (see my translation and introduction in the Penguin Classics edition pp. 155–244) and Chaucer himself. As if to clinch the matter of suggestion beyond doubt, the poet takes us into the mind of Gawain (ll. 1284–7) and reminds us that

> He was less love-laden because of the loss he must
>> Now face –
> His destruction by the stroke,
> For come it must was the case.

There is little need further to demonstrate that Gawain is not suggestible to sexual temptation. It is his courtesy that is hard pressed, not his sexual instinct, by each assault of the Lady. Even her almost desperate third throw, he deflects into the Platonic bliss of love-talk; the poet's didactic comment (ll. 1768–9),

> And peril would have impended
> Had Mary not minded her knight

plainly states that Mary did mind her knight, who accordingly felt none of the stings of concupiscence. The exposed beauty, propinquity, charm and blandishments of the Lady did not, on the evidence of the poem, illicitly suffuse either his flesh or his spirit for an instant. Thus there is no real sexual interest in the poem because the hero simply does not play that game.

It is when the Lady makes advances to him in public that he seems most upset, not because his passion is kindled, but because he must at the same time neither rebuff her decisively, which would be to her public dishonour, nor imply by his own acceptance of her advances that an illicit liaison between them is in existence or in prospect. That is why he is upset (ll. 1658–63):

In a bewitchingly well-mannered way she made up to him,
Secretly soliciting the stalwart knight
So that he was astounded, and upset in himself.
But his upbringing forbade him to rebuff her utterly,
So he behaved towards her honourably, whatever aspersions might
        Be cast.

The Lady has maintained a barrage of suggestion, and managed to
get her intended victim to enjoy delectation: but not the delectation
she wanted him to enjoy – the contemplation of making love to her.
Gawain's delectation arises from the spiritual rather than from the
sensual element in courtly love; he is delighted by her beauty and her
love-talking. The moment anything sensual is in prospect, he deflects
it by pretending not to have heard, or by interpreting it in a more or
less Platonic sense. By thus rejecting the sensual, he saves his own life.
This is the teaching of the poem. 'Life and all that makes it worth-
while, the story says, depends on the control of sexual desire', writes
D. S. Brewer (Bibliography 5, p. 73), noting the connection in the
poem between sex and death, rather than between sex and life.

How different is Gawain's behaviour when, the Lady having given
up hope either of seducing him or of persuading him to accept a love-
token, he is offered a life-protecting charm! Suggestion, delectation
and consent smoothly follow each other in his mind, and even the
Lady's express reference to the need for Gawain to hide the gift from
her husband (ll. 1862–3), which ought to have brought sharply to
Gawain's attention his duty of maintaining good faith with his host,
does not make him pause for a moment.

At the final confrontation between hero and antagonist, each ex-
presses a different view about Gawain's failure in faith. The Green
Knight admires Gawain's performance so much that he uses the poet's
favourite symbol of purity to describe him, and judiciously assesses
his shortcoming as quite minor, because respectably motivated (ll.
2364–8):

> As the pearl to the white pea in precious worth,
> So in good faith is Gawain to other gay knights.

But here your faith failed you, you flagged somewhat, sir,
Yet it was not for a well-wrought thing, nor for wooing either,
But for love of your life, which is less blameworthy.

Gawain, the sinner, naturally sees his fault in its full moral complexity, as something which threatens the whole of his knightly being (ll. 2374–84). First he accuses himself of cowardice – fear of death. Next he accuses himself of covetousness – desire to keep possession of life. These two, he says, corrupted his nature

And the liberality and loyalty belonging to chivalry.

His free-hearted spirit was corrupted by the need for subterfuge in concealing the gift of the girdle; in which act, his loyalty to his host necessarily disappeared. Gawain thus sees his sin in the orthodox manner enjoined by medieval penitential doctrine. One sin leads to another, unless real penitence and penance follow. The proof that Gawain's penitence was genuine, and that he had plainly done penance at the point of the Green Knight's axe, is that (l. 2484)

The hurt he had had in his neck was healed.

Perhaps too much has been made of Gawain's subsidiary shortcomings at the time of his shame. But they are worth a moment's attention because they help the reader to focus on the poet's attitude to Gawain's fault, which is broadly the same as that of the Green Knight and that of the 'lords and ladies belonging to the Round Table'. There is comfort for his shame, praise for his behaviour, and good-natured laughter at his discomfiture. The good-natured laughter of the poet shows in the absurdity and credibility of Gawain's actions after being accused. His fury and shame and his flinging of the green girdle from him lead naturally to his single outburst of self-exculpation (ll. 2410–28), during which listeners are treated to the exquisite pleasure of hearing Gawain, the legendary lover, condemn the whole of womankind for their sleights in a clearly monkish manner. The hero's subsequent assumption of humility, and his promise to wear the girdle as a reminder of his fault and a safeguard against pride, sit better at the end of the poem on these minor human fallibilities than they could have done on, for example, immediate, shocked, devout penitence.

It has often been said that Gawain is nowhere in the poem described, as the Green Knight is, and that the reason for this is that there is no need to describe one of the most famous heroes of Romance. But the annotation of his moral predicaments and behaviour throughout the poem describes him all the time as a complex and credible human being trying to live by certain personal standards, and nowhere more so than at and after the time when he faces his single faulty action and its consequences. But we are not left at the end just with the hero and his agonized penitence; we go away with an urbane and compassionate joke at his expense. His baldric, which he wanted to wear for ever as a mark of shame, is rated differently by his peers (ll. 2519–20):

> So it ranked as renown to the Round Table,
> And an everlasting honour to him who had it.

Gawain's reaction to this casual overthrow of his laboriously constructed scheme of guilt and remorse is not recorded: it is all very delightful, very polite, very moral, and very comically serious.

The Poem as a Play

Sir Gawain and the Green Knight was presented by the Tyneside Theatre Company at the University Theatre, Newcastle, at Christmas 1971. The final text as performed was an adaptation of this one, almost entirely by selection by Peter Stevens, with suggestions for inclusion by Michael Bogdanov, the director. The latter determined the final text, for which I wrote additional lines, working with him and the company at rehearsal. The music and lyrics were composed by Iwan Williams, and the designer was Stephanie Howard. The production was the company's best box-office success of the season. I include this account of it not only because it was an original theatrical event, but because some of the dramatic problems presented, the thinking about them and the attempts to solve them by Michael Bogdanov, throw light on the poem as literature.

Presenting what after adaptation remained essentially a narrative poem demanded above all that a convention be established which was at once valid as a vehicle for thematic treatment of the material, and flexible enough to absorb rapid flow from scene to scene, and from the minutiae of relationship and individual psychology to public spectacle and wild outdoor activity. Of this unifying action convention which he devised, Michael Bogdanov writes:

> For a long time it had appeared to me that the various parts of the poem contained strong ethnic references that have been handed down to us not merely in story form, but in song and dance form as well. Your own note refers to Cuchulain and the Beheading Game – a sequence which is contained in a sword dance called Grenoside. Strictly speaking this is a dance where a fox is beheaded and the head rolls off. There are several others which are also concerned with beheading but this one I considered to be the most appropriate for the particular dramatic sequence

of the beheading of Gawain.* It is a long-sword dance from Grenoside in Sheffield. At the same time the Pentangle theme (and song) is one that is contained in most sword dances, although many have variants according to the number of swords used, but specifically the Northumbrian Rapper dance, peculiar to Tyneside. A dance devised by the miners using the two-handled swords with which they scrape down the pit ponies, seemed the natural dance to celebrate the Pentangle description with. So gradually a form began to emerge in my mind that contained specific Northumbrian origins, particularly as the feeling in the poem, although it makes reference to the Wirral, fits perfectly some of the wild Anglo-Saxon (or Norse) conditions that exist to this day in parts of Northumberland. Add to this the haunting sound of the Northumbrian pipe which was used in the forest sequences and a feeling begins to emerge. The main source of inspiration for all the music was folk, particularly pipes, whistles and the boran† – rough-edged in other words, and the use of medieval carols – an unpublished version of the Boar's Head Carol for example. I used this very strong ethnic folk element to help bring out the rugged, wild but beautiful quality of the poem. Given this form, it was then impossible to indulge in complete medieval pageantry, and a simple image was necessary to carry both the pagan ritualistic element of fighting and dancing on the one hand, and visual images without tapestries on the other. Filching the idea of Japanese and Persian stick theatre, I decided that staves, of varying lengths, were the answer. They were used for cross-stick fighting, waving trees, stretchers, tangled woods, gates, the castle drawbridge and pinnacles, practical steps and even leashes for hounds. In other words, a stick is a stick is a stick until the imagination animates it. Stick dancing,

*This 'long-sword dance' was danced while Gawain lay tossing uneasily (ll. 2006–8) before getting up to go to the Green Chapel. The dancers made the 'Knot' of the Pentangle around his drowsing head with their swords as he half-knelt, and unmade it with a sudden movement which gave the effect of decapitation, and made Gawain fall headlong awake from his nightmare – a beautiful dramatic stroke which is absolutely true to the poem. – B.S.

†The boran is an Irish skin drum, often played with the knuckles. – B.S.

stick fighting, stick images and you have the second element of the production. The final one is that of colour – a dominant theme in the poem. Colour and cloths. The Round Table becomes symbolic – a series of cushions in a circle. The bed becomes cloths and cushions laid on the ground and the costumes become tunics and tights all vividly bright in tie-dyed colours. Cloths and sticks united to form banners become the surround of the stage. So there you have it. Sticks, cloths, dances, folk song and colour – the basic components of the production.

Michael Bogdanov wrote that when I asked him how he arrived at his unifying action convention, and so he does not describe how the whole action was carried along on the actual words of the poem, faithfully and well spoken by an intelligent cast who responded remarkably to the challenge presented by alliterative verse.

In the Introduction (p. 17) I mentioned the medieval technique of 'interlace' which the poet used in alternating between the hunting and wooing episodes. In the stage production, this technique was enhanced with frequent cutting of the action from hunt to bedchamber and back again, while the locale of both remained on-stage. That is, the bed with recumbent knight and tempting Lady was a feature of the landscape, so that, for example, the panicking deer leapt over the astounded knight, and the narrator, kneeling forestage while the hunt wheeled round him, could cock his head in the direction of the Lady shamelessly essaying the knight while he read the lines:

For the noble prince had expressly prohibited
Meddling with male deer in the months of close season. (ll. 1156–7)

The banners of sticks and cloths ranged round the stage became trees and thickets for the quarry to dodge into and out of in their three different styles. Of the interweaving of the hunting and wooing, which was for me the most brilliant achievement in the production, Michael Bogdanov writes:

I wanted to integrate at certain dramatic moments bursts of the hunt and climaxes in the wooing so that I could juxtapose the hunting of the man with the hunting of the animals. Although it does not closely follow this pattern in the poem, nevertheless there is sufficient parallel to make it dramatically possible, and I attempted to mirror all the time. Once again the sticks played important parts as spears or battens, knives or poles between which slaughtered animals were slung. This brings me to a final element which was used in the production – that of tumbling. First of all, in using the human body as an instrument, it seemed important to me to evolve a convention that, without being balletic, encompassed both the agility of an animal and the theatrical celebration of the art of an actor. A fox runs, a boar fights, a deer leaps and jumps, but to try and depict this naturalistically leads to a confusion of styles. Therefore the boar was able to beat off attackers with karate throws, the deer was able to do hand-spins and neck-flips, the fox was able to somersault over the backs and shoulders of crouching actors. In the opening sequences while the actors were coming into the auditorium, showing in the words of Peter Brook 'that we have nothing up our sleeves', the actors indulged in a series of acrobatics, tricks and stick fights as an appetiser for what would come. The beasts and monsters met by Gawain on his northward journey were overcome in a completely acrobatic way, for the play always had a unity of style. So the mental acrobatics of Gawain and the Lady were mirrored by the physical acrobatics of animals being hunted.

All that, to my mind, perfectly accords with the essence of the poem. Not surprisingly in the light of it, the programme acknowledges the services of two physical education experts as well as leaders of morris- and sword-dance groups. The first week of rehearsal was taken up entirely with athletics and dancing: actors are traditionally among the most hard-working professional people, but the successful tackling of this kind of task in a company working a three-week repertory is altogether extraordinary.

I asked Michael Bogdanov to tell me how he arrived at one other important detail in his production. This concerned Morgan, whose function he asked me to describe in additional lines which were spoken as a kind of prologue, and who appeared throughout the play as the instigator of every trial to which Gawain was subjected, even the battles in the wilderness on his way north. His answer would have pleased Mother Angela Carson, O.S.U., who considers Morgan as the principle of unity in the poem (see Bibliography 15). It was essential for the audience to know the source of Gawain's trials from the outset, to be told what the unfolding conflict was about and to be given the chance to identify with the right character.

It seemed to me that for the stage the one dramatic element that was essential for the full theatrical effect of the poem to be realized was the direct apposition of the forces of good and evil. Good as represented by Gawain, but *not* evil as represented by the Green Knight, who after all is only an instrument of evil. Therefore the shadowy figure who is referred to on a number of occasions but named only once late in the poem, that is Morgan the Fay, needed to become a fully-fledged person, if the central struggle in which good triumphs over evil was to be set up. As she has no lines, the task became one of symbolic integration. Therefore Morgan was seen to control or was seen to be vanquished, triumphant, happy, sad, frustrated etc., at various points in Gawain's journeys. Were I to do it again I would extend this role even further. In one sense I was only carrying through the old pantomine tradition of the Witch and Knight. In another, like Prospero, to demonstrate that no matter how much we consider we are in control of our own destinies, there is always the demonic which is beyond our control. Anyway magic or bewitching must always be seen to have a source, as the intervention of the completely supernatural for children is something horrific.

Michael Bogdanov was right. Sir Gawain is a Christmas festival poem, and his production was a Christmas show infinitely superior to pantomime, though it had to fulfil, and did fulfil, one of the main purposes of a pantomime, which is to stir and delight children.

The Manuscript

Sir Gawain and the Green Knight exists in a single vellum manuscript measuring only about seven inches by five. It is the last of four poems on the manuscript, the other three being *Pearl*, *Cleanness* and *Patience*. The manuscript is in the Cotton Collection in the British Museum, and used to be bound with two unrelated manuscripts as M S Cotton Nero A.x, 'but was rebound separately in November 1964, and now bears the distinguishing mark Art. 3 on spine and fly-leaf' (Davis, p. i).

The writing, which is in the same hand throughout except possibly for the motto at the end (see Gollancz, p. 132), is late fourteenth century, and not only has the ink faded, but some of the pages were closed before the ink was dry: hence the great difficulty of reading the poem, although many of the blurred letters have been interpreted by reading the blotted impression with a mirror. The language is agreed to be North Midland or, more especially, the dialect of Cheshire and South Lancashire.

The manuscript is illustrated by twelve pictures, four of which represent scenes from *Sir Gawain*. Only one of these, which shows Gawain lying in bed and the Lady touching the end of his beard with the middle finger of her left hand, is at all clear. Since the details of the picture do not correspond exactly with any situation described in the poem, and the artist is an inferior one, it is of little interest.

Theories about the Poet

IT is not known who the poet of *Sir Gawain and the Green Knight* was, although several names have been suggested at various times and subsequently discarded. Cargill and Schlauch ('The Pearl and its Jeweler', P.M.L.A. xliii, 105–23), taking as departure point the similarity in style between *Pearl* and *Sir Gawain*, suggest that the infant girl lamented in *Pearl* was Margaret, daughter of the Earl of Pembroke and granddaughter of Edward III, and that the poet was accordingly one of Pembroke's clerks, perhaps John Donne or John Prat. A much earlier suggestion, based on the writing at the beginning of *Sir Gawain*, in a fifteenth-century hand, of 'Hugo de', was that the poet was the Scottish author of alliterative romance, Huchown: but the style of surviving works attributed to Huchown is quite different. Gollancz (Medieval Library 1921, pp. xlvi–l) proposed Ralph Strode, the Oxford scholastic philosopher and logician, and C. O. Chapman ('The Authorship of *Pearl*', P.M.L.A. xlvii, 346–53) John of Erghome, but neither of these suggestions has been accepted.

The most interesting suggestion to me is that made by Ormerod Greenwood in the introduction to his verse translation published by the Lion and Unicorn Press in 1956. The full evidence, with its basis in Numerology (which had high standing in medieval times), textual puns and provenance, is too long to be given in full, but I summarize Greenwood's findings.

Hugh Mascy, or Hugo de Masci, is the conjectured name. The Masseys are an old Cheshire family ('as many Massies as asses' is a local tag quoted by Greenwood), with which is associated, a century later, the manuscript of *St Erkenwald*, a fifth poem often ascribed to the *Sir Gawain* poet (see my translation in the Penguin Classics, *The Owl and the Nightingale, Cleanness, St Erkenwald* pp. 11–43). The geography of *Sir Gawain* firmly links it with the Massey district, and the names Hugo and Margery (the latter, which means pearl, being the name of the child mourned in *Pearl*) abound in the Massey family in the fourteenth century.

The numerological evidence of authorship is found chiefly in *Pearl* which, like *Sir Gawain*, has a hundred and one stanzas. The numerical value, in the medieval alphabet, of the letters in the name Hugo de Masci, is 101, and the seal inscriptions of the family, ending with the name *Masci*, end CI, or 101. The arrangement of *Pearl*, which begins with twelve groups of five stanzas each of twelve lines, and its total number of lines, 1212, takes on further meaning when considered with the fact that the name Margery Masci has twelve letters, and that there are significantly placed puns on the word 'Masci' in the poem. Ormerod Greenwood thus finds the family name 'Masci', the name of the daughter 'Margery' and the name of the poet 'Hugo de' hammered home in a series of puns and numerical values throughout the extraordinarily complicated structure of the poem. This structure seems to me only to make sense from the point of view of the poet and his public if some key, such as that suggested, will unlock its secret. But, as Ormerod Greenwood writes, his attribution must remain short of proof 'until a Hugh can be found with a daughter Margery who died in infancy'.

The Pentangle and its Significance

THE Pentangle, or five-pointed star, which may be drawn without taking the pen from the paper (hence 'The Endless Knot'), is assigned to Sir Gawain only in this poem. Elsewhere in Romance, his shield bears one of the usual heraldic creatures – a lion, gryphon or eagle – in gold upon green. It is quite clear that the poet attaches special importance to the Pentangle, for three reasons. Firstly, the section on Gawain's shield beginning at line 619 has a coloured initial: apart from the big coloured initials which editors have usually taken as marking the four main divisions of the poem, there are only five of these smaller coloured initials in the whole poem. Secondly, by explaining in detail what the Pentangle is physically, he acknowledges his audience's probable ignorance of it and attests its historical importance. When he writes

> ... the English call it,
> In all the land, I hear, the Endless Knot

he is merely using the medieval poet's common method of authenticating new material – that is, by pretending that the new material is traditional. (In fact, there is no other mention of the word in English until 1646, although the pentacular figure appears occasionally 'as an ornament in manuscripts and on churches' (Davis, p. 93).) And perhaps two folk references should be taken into account: the Pentangle seems at some time to have been known as 'The Druid's Foot', though I cannot date this reference; also English folk dancers, at the end of one sword-dance, interlock their wooden swords in the form of a pentangle, hold it up and cry, 'A Nut! A Nut!' (Knot). The third and chief proof of the Pentangle's importance in the poem is the carefully detailed explanation of its emblematic significance, which I discuss below after summarizing some of the traditions about the device with which the poet may have been familiar.

The Pentangle, the most important sign in magic, the quintessence of the alchemists, is about as old as history. It is first found scratched on Babylonian pottery from Ur, and from then onward figures prominently in oriental and near eastern religions as a mystic symbol of perfection. The Pythagoreans used it, probably because five is the perfect number, being the marriage of the first masculine number, three, with the first feminine number, two (unity not being a true number). In one of the Gnostic systems it was the passport to the Kingdom of Light: the Virgin Sophia would admit to her realm only bearers of the seal of the Pentangle. In the Tarot pack, which is used for divination, it survives as an alternative to the Dish, one of the four suits (Jessie Weston, in *From Ritual to Romance*, suggests that it is a female fertility symbol), and it also figures in Freemasonry on account of its association with Solomon. Its special functions appear to have been as a guardian of health and protector against demons.

According to Jewish legends about Solomon, there is no justification for assigning the Pentangle to his seal: the Jewish Encyclopaedia says that it is only in Arabic continuations of the legends that the early, primitive Pentangle occurs, and that it is these versions that reached the West. But Sir E. A. Wallis-Budge (*Amulets and Superstitions*) suggests that the hexagram, or in Jewish parlance the Magen David, is a later modification of the Pentangle or Pentacle. However, the Pentacle, containing the ineffable name of God – YHWH (Yahweh or Jehovah) – does appear in the Kabbalah, and representations of it occasionally figure in synagogues. A friend of mine interested in such things writes: 'I've a feeling that in his *degenerate* days Solomon used the five-pointed star as a defence against demons – neglecting thus the spiritual device of his father's "Star of David".' All this fits together. But 'Star' has crept into the terminology only because of the shape of the two devices: the word 'magen' in 'Magen David' means 'protector', not 'star'. A protector is a shield, and of the two general forms of the device, the elongated and the regular, the former appears to be best fitted for working on a shield 'royally in red gold upon red gules'.

So this mysterious device, magical in its antecedents and emblematic of vaguely suggested powers, was taken by this didactic poet and given a precise significance as the emblem of his hero, in lines 623–65.

He stresses that it is a 'new' Pentangle because he attaches new values to it. These are, as Robert W. Ackerman explains (Bibliography 10, p. 257), 'not a random collection of Christian pentads, such as the five wounds and the five joys', but a carefully complete statement of doctrine and devotion relevant to the meaning of the poem, and especially to the spiritual status of the hero. Ackerman (pp. 257–64) mentions frequent references in fourteenth-century 'penitential doctrine' to the misuse of the five wits and the five fingers. As for the five qualities listed and inter-related in lines 651–61, together they make up the 'holy truth' (ME trawþe, line 626) which the Pentangle betokens, the composite quality of perfection against which Gawain's eventual fault, faithlessness (ME vntrawþe, line 2509, of which the green girdle is the token), must be measured.

Notes on Arthurian Matters

Gawain

Gawain apparently begins as an Irish hero. His father, King Lot of the Orkneys, has been traced through Welsh Lloch to the Irish god Lug, Cuchulain's father, who was the colour of the setting sun from sunset to sunrise. In the early stories Gawain's strength, like that of Cuchulain, the hero of the Beheading Game in *Fled Bricrend*, increases until midday and then declines towards evening, and he inherits from the Irish hero his diadem and golden hair. In Welsh legend, before the Arthurian cycle developed, there is a Gwri Gwalltenryn 'of the golden hair', who passes on this characteristic to Gwalchmai, the Welsh Gawain. Possibly Gwalchmai was hero of a pre-Arthurian cycle of adventures, and so became easily identified with the new hero. But Robert Graves in *The White Goddess* notes that Gwalchmai ('hawk of May'), Gwalchaved ('hawk of summer'), and Gwalch gwyn ('white hawk') are mystical names, and that the Welsh court-bards always compared their royal patrons to hawks: he says the last two names are respectively early forms of Galahad and Gawain. The hawk is of course a sun-bird. Another primitive solar characteristic of Gawain's, of which there is one possible echo (l. 861) in our poem, is his eternal youth. This he received as a gift when he visited the fairy island inhabited only by women, which in Irish tradition sometimes represents the other world.

In the Grail romances, and as Gwalchmai in the Welsh Triads, Gawain is persistently represented as a healer well versed in herbal remedies. Jessie Weston, in *From Ritual to Romance*, sees Gawain as the medicine man who, in the fertility ritual underlying the mystery of the Grail, restores to life the spirit of vegetation. Brought up on Malory, we may forget that Gawain was the original Grail hero, and that the story on which Chrétien de Troyes and others based their Grail romances was a non-Christian Grail poem by the Welshman Bleheris. The Church was opposed to the Grail stories.

In early medieval Romance Gawain, not Arthur, was the owner of the light-giving sword Excalibur. He became the pattern of chivalry and courtesy and, like many popular heroes, became the subject of satirical tales as well as heroic adventures. Chrétien de Troyes makes him a dallier, too ready to champion girls irrespective of the merits of their cases. But he never has an illicit affair, as Lancelot and Tristan do. In one Romance, in order to save King Arthur's life, he weds and treats chivalrously the foul hag Ragnell, who, not unexpectedly, turns into a beautiful girl.

In the English Arthurian poems and satires Gawain virtually becomes a national hero. William of Malmesbury (d. about 1143) records the existence of his tomb at Ross in Pembrokeshire, and all the English Romancers, from Geoffrey of Monmouth to our poet, rank him first among Arthur's knights. 'Gavin' is still a popular name in Scotland and the north of England, and Gawain's skull, as Terence Tiller reminds us,* is of course in Dover Castle.

Morgan the Fay

The title 'goddess' (l. 2452), which is first found applied to Morgan in Giraldus Cambrensis, the twelfth-century Welsh writer, shows her to be related to the Irish goddess of battle, Morrigu, who opposed Cuchulain with her enchantments just as Morgan opposes Arthur and his court – interruptedly and often ambiguously. Her warlike attributes are preserved in the story of Sir Peredur, who was trained in arms by nine sorceresses. She has been traced farther back still, to the Celtic goddess Matrona, who was worshipped from northern Italy to the mouth of the Rhine and gave her name to the Marne. Her connection with water is found everywhere. The mermaids of the Breton coast, who entice fishermen, either killing them with their watery embraces or dragging them down to a kind of hellish eternal bliss in their submarine palaces, are Morgans. Morgan is also related to the Welsh lake fairies who, having ensnared their human lovers, lay pro-

*In the talk discussed on p. 153.

hibitions on them, and desert them when the prohibitions are broken. One especially sinister manifestation which may underlie the many references to her appearing, as in *Sir Gawain and the Green Knight*, as an ugly old woman, is the Welsh Gwrach y Rhibyn, a hideous hag dressed in black, who may be seen by water, splashing herself, or dipping and raising herself in a pool.

But one of the Welsh fairies, called Modron, has healing powers, which may account for the last role of Morgan in Arthur's supposed lifetime. Readers of Malory will remember that she is one of the three mourning queens who come by barge to take away the dying king. When in their care, Arthur tells Sir Bedivere, 'I will into the vale of Avilion to heal me of my grievous wound.' Morgan's enmity to the Round Table is variously accounted for. One tradition places the blame on Guinevere, whose adultery with Lancelot threatens the whole civilization of King Arthur's court, which gives Morgan, as sister of the King, a clearly moral function. She gives Arthur a magic drink which opens his eyes to his wife's betrayal of him with one of his feudal subjects. According to another tradition, Guinevere initiated the hostility by exposing Morgan's intrigue with the knight Guiomar. In all the stories, as well as in *Sir Gawain and the Green Knight*, Morgan especially hates Guinevere, who was responsible for her banishment from the court. She built a valley chapel from which none who had been untrue in love, having entered, could escape. The Green Chapel may owe its origin to a memory of this, for it was specifically to test the chastity of Arthur's knights, which she delighted in attacking, that Morgan built her chapel. That double role of temptress and scourge of those who fall to her temptation is played in our poem both by Morgan and by all members of her scheme of enchantment. In addition, these enchanters seem to approve those who resist them.

This triple activity is appropriate to a goddess who, as Terence Tiller points out, has a name which means 'offspring of the sea', and is in fact 'a love goddess: Aphrodite'. Not surprisingly, the Christian Romancers see her ugliness and great age Platonically, and attribute them to her dealings with the devil. She came by her '*chair ridée*' and '*mamelles pendantes*' through lechery and black magic. But our poet, allowing her to retain youth in one of her manifestations, recognizes her grace and beauty. She is a complex and ambiguous goddess, fit to test such a knight as Gawain.

King Arthur and Camelot

There are two schools of thought about Arthur. One, as represented by Sir Edmund Chambers in his *Arthur of Britain* (1927, reissued by Sidgwick & Jackson 1966), says that he was a fifth- or sixth-century British general who fought against the Saxons, became a racial hero, and attracted to himself during the Middle Ages a whole range of mythical and magical exploits appropriate to a national hero. The other school finds the attribution of historical reality to Arthur flimsily based upon pseudo-historians who lived much later, and prefers to think of him, on the evidence of a mass of early literature, as in origin basically a Celtic nature-god with attributes connecting him with the sun. I find that Chambers and those who think like him protest too much, and am more interested in the kind of evidence and argument expressed by Terence Tiller in a radio talk of February 1972 called *The Road to Camelot*.

Tiller noted the wide range of characteristics Arthur shares with minor sun-deities of other cultures, of the early Mediterranean and even of the orient. He is a boar-hunter like Theseus and Hercules and the Mycenean heroes; he is wounded in the thigh (euphemism for testicles) like Adonis and, if the Waste Land of Grail Romance, which is barren because he is impotent, is to blossom again, he must be healed by a virgin knight – either Percival or Galahad – who bears a (phallic) bloodstained lance. Tiller remarked that in Otranto Cathedral there is a representation of 'Arthur mounted on a goat and carrying the unmistakable phallic club of the Sun-hero Hercules', and encircled by the Zodiac; just as Glastonbury was once encircled by a vast system of landscape gardening that represents the Zodiac.

If Arthur was a historical figure of the post-Roman period, it seems to me impossible that so many parts of the country should claim him and Camelot for their own: Caerleon-upon Usk in Monmouthshire, Camelford in Cornwall, Queen's Camel, Glastonbury, Cadbury Castle in Somerset, and Winchester in Hampshire. Even in Scotland, 'Dumbarton itself is called Castrum Arthuri in a record in 1367' (Chambers, pp. 190–91). And all over the west of these islands, there are place-names which include the name Arthur. It is altogether too much. The poet does not place Camelot; but if Gawain's route from court to the Wirral is to be imagined at all, Camelot should be in the West Country or South Wales, and not southern England. The huge hill-fortress at South Cadbury with eighteen acres raised 150 feet above the valley floor, and ramparts thirty-five feet high, the biggest late Celtic one in the West Country, seems as likely a place as any if Camelot was ever a real place. But the civilization exposed by digs of Celtic sites is a simple rural one, quite unlike the sophisticated one represented at Camelot in medieval Romances, which is an idealized contemporary one.

Merlin

'Merlin seems to have been wholly a creation of Geoffrey [of Monmouth – B.S.]'s brain', writes Chambers (p. 95), but goes on to recognize that Celticists give him a much earlier provenance and associate him with an early Welsh prophet Myrrdin. What seems clear is that, once he became established through Geoffrey as the wizard of Arthur's court, Merlin naturally attracted to himself much of the common stock of wizardry from religion and from European and oriental folklore. Geoffrey (d. 1154) credits him with having brought the Giant's Dance (Stonehenge) from Ireland to its present site, and having been instrumental in the begetting of Arthur upon Igraine, wife of Gorlois of Cornwall, by Uther Pendragon. In Malory he is the one who arranged the sword-in-the-stone test for Arthur's succession, and in another account he made the Round Table, which had originally belonged to Uther, but did not come to Arthur until

Guinevere brought it as a dowry, together with a hundred knights.

Merlin's supernatural powers are explained by his having no mortal for a father, his parents having been a nun and a devil. Robert de Borron, the French poet, who based his *Merlin* largely on a version of Geoffrey of Monmouth's work, grafted on to the wizard a traditional legend about the begetting of the Antichrist. Accordingly, in some works Merlin is a Power of Darkness. He has been linked with a Breton wizard, and conjectured as the cultural descendant of a British god who was worshipped at Stonehenge. He even becomes a figure in Scots folklore; in the ballad of *Childe Rowland* he is a warlock who rescues King Arthur's daughter from Fairyland. He survived as a figure in popular legend, and is twice mentioned by Shakespeare.

As far as *Sir Gawain* is concerned, we are interested in Merlin as the ultimate source of the magic power which is used to test the hero. Everyone would know that he became the lover and teacher of Morgan the Fay when the latter fled from Camelot in disgrace; and it is stated in the poem that she used the potency taught her by the 'susceptible sage' with the malignant intention of trying Arthur's court and terrifying Guinevere to death. So, since Merlin taught it to Morgan only because 'she lavished fervent love' on him, the poet establishes a precise connection between malign potency and lechery. His attack on illicit sex in this poem is incidental but in *Cleanness* (translated in *The Owl and the Nightingale, Cleanness, St Erkenwald*, Penguin Classics 1971) he sermonizes on it in elaborate obsessive detail.

Extracts from the Original Poem

FIT I, STANZA 9: *The green hair of the knight and his horse*

Wel gay watʒ þis gome   gered in grene
& þe here of his hed   of his hors swete;
Fayre fannand fax   vmbefoldes his schulderes;
A much berd as a busk   ouer his brest henges,
Þat wyth his hiʒlich here,   þat of his hed reches,
Watʒ euesed al vmbetorne,   abof his elbowes,
Þat half his armes þer-vnder   were halched in þe wyse
Of a kyngeʒ capados,   þat closes his swyre.
Þe mane of þat mayn hors   much to hit lyke,
Wel cresped & cemmed   wyth knottes ful mony,
Folden in wyth fildore   aboute þe fayre grene,
Ay a herle of þe here,   an oþer of golde;
Þe tayl & his toppyng   twynnen of a sute,
& bounden boþe wyth a bande   of a bryʒt grene,
Dubbed wyth ful dere stoneʒ,   as þe dok lasted;
Syþen þrawen wyth a þwong,   a þwarle-knot alofte,
Þer mony belleʒ ful bryʒt   of brende golde rungen.
Such a fole upon folde,   ne freke þat hym rydes,
Watʒ neuer sene in þat sale   wyth syʒt er þat tyme,
        With yʒe.
    He loked as layt so lyʒt,
    So sayd al þat hym syʒe;
    Hit semed as no mon myʒt
    Vnder his dyntteʒ dryʒe.

FIT II, STANZA 31: *Sir Gawain's northward journey*

Mony klyf he ouerclambe   in contrayeʒ straunge,

Fer floten fro his frendeȝ   fremedly he rydeȝ.
At vche warþe oþer water   þer þe wyȝe passed,
He fonde a foo hym before,   bot ferly hit were,
& þat so foule & so felle   þat feȝt hym byhode.
So mony meruayl bi mount   þer þe mon fyndeȝ,
Hit were to tore for to telle   of þe tenþe dole.
Sumwhyle wyth wormeȝ he werreȝ,   & with wolues als,
Sumwhyle wyth wodwos   þat woned in þe knarreȝ,
Boþe wyth bulleȝ & bereȝ   & boreȝ oþerquyle,
& etayneȝ þat hum anelede,   of þe heȝe felle;
Nade he ben duȝty & dryȝe   & dryȝtyn had serued,
Douteles he hade ben ded   & dreped ful ofte.
For werre wrathed hym not so much,   þat wynter was wors,
When þe colde cler water   fro þe cloudez schadde,
& fres er hit falle myȝt   to þe fale erþe;
Ner slayn wyth þe slete   he sleped in his yrnes
Mo nyȝteȝ þen innoghe   in naked rokkeȝ,
Þer as claterande fro þe crest   þe colde borne renneȝ,
& henged heȝe ouer his hede   in hard ysse-ikkles.
Þus in peryl & payne   & plytes ful harde
Bi contray cayreȝ þis knyȝt   tyl krystmasse euen,
   Al one;
  Þe knyȝt wel þat tyde
  To Mary made his mone,
  Þat ho hym red to ryde
  & wysse hym so sum wone.

FIT III, STANZA 49: *The Lady's first visit to Sir Gawain*

'God moroun, sir Gawayn,'   sayde þat gay lady,
'ȝe are a sleper vnslyȝe,   þat mon may slyde hider.
Now are ȝe tan astyt,   bot true vs may schape,

I schal bynde yow in your bedde, þat be ʒe trayst.'
Al laʒande þe lady lauced þo bourdeʒ.
'Goud moroun, gay,' quoþ Gawayn þe blyþe,
Me schal worþe at your wille, & þat me wel lykeʒ,
For I ʒelde me ʒederly & ʒeʒe after grace,
& þat is þe best, by my dome, for me byhoueʒ nede.'
& þus he bourded aʒayn with mony a blyþe laʒter.
'Bot wolde ʒe, lady louely, þen leue me grante,
& deprece your prysoun & pray hym to ryse,
I wolde boʒe of þis bed & busk me better,
I schulde keuer þe more comfort to karp yow wyth.'
'Nay, for soþe, beau sir,' sayd þat swete,
'ʒe schal not rise of your bedde, I rych yow better,
I schal happe yow here þat oþer half als,
& syþen karp wyth my knyʒt þat I kaʒt haue;
For I wene wel, iwysse, sir Wowen ʒe are,
Þat alle þe worlde worchipeʒ, quereso ʒe ride;
Your honour, your hendelayk is hendely praysed
With lordez, wyth ladyeʒ, with alle þat lyf bere.
& now ʒe ar here, iwysse, & we bot oure one;
My lorde & his ledeʒ ar on lenþe faren,
Oþer burneʒ in her bedde, & my burdeʒ als,
Þe dor drawen & dit with a derf haspe.
& syþen I haue in þis hous hym þat al lykeʒ,
I schal ware my whyle wel quyl hit lasteʒ,
          With tale.
      ʒe ar welcum to my cors,
      Yowre awen won to wale,
      Me behoueʒ of fyne force
      Your seruaunt be, & schale.'

Bibliographical References in the Text

1 Marie Boroff: *'Sir Gawain and the Green Knight': A Stylistic and Metrical Study* (Yale University Press, 1962)

2 Larry D. Benson: 'The Source of the Beheading Episode in *Sir Gawain and the Green Knight*', in *Modern Philology,* vol. lix, no. 1, August 1961, p. 2

3 Jessie Weston: *From Ritual to Romance* (C.U.P., 1920; Anchor Books, 1957)

4 Larry D. Benson: *Art and Tradition in 'Sir Gawain and the Green Knight'* (Rutgers University Press, 1965)

5 D. S. Brewer: 'Courtesy and the *Gawain*-Poet', in John Lawlor (ed.), *Patterns of Love and Courtesy: Essays in Memory of C. S. Lewis* (Arnold, 1966)

6 Lewis Thorpe: Geoffrey of Monmouth's *The History of the Kings of Britain* (trans.) (Penguin Classics 1966)

7 S. R. T. O. D'Ardenne: ' "The Green Count" and *Sir Gawain and the Green Knight*', in *Review of English Studies*, vol. 10, 1959.

8 D. E. Baughan: 'The Role of Morgan le Fay in Sir Gawain and the Green Knight', in *A Journal of English Literary History,* vol. 17, no. 4, December 1950

9 H. L. Savage: *The Gawain-Poet: Studies in his Personality and Background* (University of North Carolina Press, 1956)

10 Robert W. Ackerman: 'Gawain's Shield: Penitential Doctrine in *Sir Gawain and the Green Knight*', in *Anglia*, vol. 76, 1958

11 R. W. V. Elliott: 'Landscape and Rhetoric in Middle English Alliterative Poetry', in *Melbourne Critical Review*, vol. 4, 1961

12 Robert W. Ackerman: ' "Pared out of Paper": *Gawain* 802

and *Purity* 1408', in *The Journal of English and Germanic Philology*, vol. lvi, no. 3, July 1957

13 Donald R. Howard: *The Three Temptations: Medieval Man in Search of the World* (Princeton, 1966)

14 J. A. Burrow: *A Reading of 'Sir Gawain and the Green Knight'* (Routledge & Kegan Paul, 1965)

15 Mother Angela Carson, O.S.U.: 'Morgan la Fée as the Principle of Unity in *Gawain and the Green Knight*', in *Modern Language Quarterly*, vol. 23, 1962

16 Cecily Clark: '*Sir Gawain and the Green Knight*: Characterisation by Syntax', in *Essays in Criticism*, vol. xvi, no. 4, October 1966

17 Albert B. Friedman: 'Morgan le Fay in *Sir Gawain and the Green Knight*', in *Speculum*, vol. 35, 1960.

18 G. L. Kittredge: *A Study of 'Sir Gawain and the Green Knight'* (C.U.P., 1916)

19 Morton Donner: 'Tact as a Criterion of Reality in *Sir Gawain and the Green Knight*', in *Papers in English Language and Literature*, vol. 1, 1965

Bibliographical Suggestions for the Student

FACED with a bibliography which lists hundreds of study articles and scores of books on *Sir Gawain and the Green Knight*, the student may find it useful if I make some suggestions based on my own reading and experience in preparing this book, and attempt to make a balanced modest selection from the mass of criticism available.

Donald R. Howard and Christian Zacher, *Critical Studies of 'Sir Gawain and the Green Knight'* (University of Notre Dame Press, Notre Dame, Indiana and London, 1968) is a thick paperback anthology of carefully selected *Sir Gawain* criticism. In the introductory section Morton W. Bloomfield's '*Sir Gawain and the Green Knight*: an Appraisal' surveys the field of criticism judiciously and informatively. Among the critics represented in the book whom I have found especially useful are C. S. Lewis, Larry D. Benson, Marie Boroff, Donald R. Howard, A. C. Spearing and J. A. Burrow. A shortcoming of the book is that, although it includes several attacks on the anthropological approach to *Sir Gawain* of John Speirs and others, Speirs himself is not represented. Speir's work on the poem (pp. 215–51 of *Medieval English Poetry: the Non-Chaucerian Tradition*) I regard as essential reading, because it is committed and detailed criticism in which the poem is seen as a product of a whole civilization. The student will have to make up his mind, as I have done, about the extent and importance of the underlying pagan ritual described by Speirs.

Of the study articles I have quoted, I recommend numbers 2, 5, 10, 11, 15, 16 and 17 listed in my Bibliographical References in the Text; and of the books, numbers 1, 3, 4, 9, 13, 14.

Of these books, I should like especially to recommend three. Marie Boroff's '*Sir Gawain and the Green Knight*': *A Stylistic and Metrical Study* appears from its title to be a dauntingly technical work, but it opens a serious and satisfactory way into the heart of the poem, and is distinguished by its combination of close attention to detail and sure aesthetic sense. Larry D. Benson's *Art and Tradition in 'Sir Gawain and the Green Knight'* is excellent on the tone and background of the poem, and has a particularly illuminating chapter on 'Literary Convention and Characterization in *Sir Gawain*'. J. A. Burrow, in his *A Reading of 'Sir Gawain and the Green Knight'*, always appears to see the poem whole: his balance and commitment seem to me admirable. I found it useful to consider excellent specialist articles like Morton Donner's 'Tact as a Criterion of Reality in *Sir Gawain and the Green Knight*' (Bibliography 19), D. S. Brewer's 'Courtesy and the *Gawain-Poet*' (Bibliography 5), and the section in Donald R. Howard's book (Bibliography 13) entitled 'Chivalry and the Pride of Life' in the light of Burrow's overall view.

Of other books, Charles Moorman's *The Pearl-Poet* (Twayne, 1968) is a survey of all the work attributed to the author of *Sir Gawain*, and is based on very wide reading. John Gardner in his introduction to *The Complete Works of the Gawain-Poet* (University of Chicago, 1965) usefully emphasizes the homogeneity of the four poems in the Cotton manuscript, but readers should be warned against accepting his translation as necessarily faithful ('... I have introduced new but consistent imagery ...' – p. viii).

A poem of such complexity as *Sir Gawain and the Green Knight* seems to me never to receive useful or even fair treatment in general literary histories, and so I warn the serious student against them. But there is a good essay by Dorothy Everett on 'The Alliterative Revival' (Chapter III of her *Essays on Medieval Literature*, OUP, 1955), and a valuable book on the whole genre of Romance and its background in Eugene Vinaver's *The Rise of Romance* (OUP, 1971).

Notes

Fit I

The manuscript bears no title, nor are the fits or stanzas numbered.

1 The poem opens with a traditional medieval literary device – the placing of the story to come in actual history. But the 'history' is a collection of legends, developed gradually since classical times, and given form and authority by such writers as Nennius and Geoffrey of Monmouth. Nennius (fl. 796) compiled his *Historia Britonum* on the geography and history of Britain and was chiefly responsible for making Arthur a historical figure, and Geoffrey of Monmouth (1100?–1154), drawing on many sources including Nennius, wrote *Historia Regum Britanniae* (The History of the Kings of Britain), a compendious and mainly fictitious work which created national king-heroes like Cymbeline, Arthur and Lear, and firmly traced English origins to heroic classical times. Romulus, Ticius and Longbeard ('Langaberde' in the text) were all legendary racial ancestors who gave their names to their peoples and countries, like Brutus. Nennius gave Longbeard the additional distinction of biblical ancestry, tracing his line back to Japhet, 'the first man after the Flood to come to Europe' (Gollancz, p. 96).

3 The story of the treachery of Antenor and Aeneas at the fall of Troy derives from pseudo-classical writings of early medieval times, purporting to be based on an account of the fall of Troy by Dares Phrygius, a Trojan priest mentioned in the Iliad, and a diary by

Dictys Cretensis, a Cretan who served with Idomeneus against Troy. The account of Troy based on these given by Guido del Colonna, a thirteenth-century Sicilian writer of Latin romances, was widely used by English and Scottish medieval writers. Gollancz thinks Antenor is specified here as 'the treacherous trickster', since Antenor took the lead in the treachery. But since Aeneas is clearly implicated (in Guido, Hecuba says to him: 'You have betrayed your country and the city in which you were born') and he is mentioned in the poem as the ancestor of Britain's founder, the opinion of Davis and Waldron that Aeneas is the trickster is to be preferred.

13   Brutus was the grandson of Aeneas, according to Nennius, but the great-grandson according to Geoffrey. Probably 'Felix' is an epithet appropriate to a founder rather than part of Brutus's name (see discussion in Davis. pp. 71–2). Brutus, according to Geoffrey, landed at Totnes, 'then called the island Britain from his own name, and his companions he called Britons ... A little later the language of the people, which had up to then been known as Trojan or Crooked Greek, was called British' (Lewis Thorpe, Bibliography 6, p. 72).

30–36   The poet tells his audience what to expect. He has a 'lay' – originally 'a short lyric or narrative poem intended to be sung' (Shorter OED) but conventionally almost any composition recited or sung by a minstrel – which is already authenticated by performance (l. 31) and the written word (l. 33). It will be spoken (ll. 31–2); it is a composition in alliterative verse (l. 35); it is a narrative (l. 36) of traditional matter (l. 34).

37   Camelot. For discussion of its location, see pp. 153–4.

40   Gollancz (p. 96) quotes evidence to show that the kind of Christmas festivity here described was characteristically English, and was not found on the continent.

47   The 'noble din' was the sound of the tournament.

54   Waldron (p. 32) suggests that the listener is being invited to consider the events of the poem as having taken place during the golden age ('prime') of Arthur's court, i.e. before any of the disasters referred to in the first stanza happened.

60   I follow Gollancz, who adds the concept 'yester' to remedy a line defective in the original; and do not understand why Davis considers that 'no satisfactory emendation has been proposed '(p. 74).

66–70   'Hondeselle', which I have translated as 'largesse', describes a New Year gift meant to express good wishes or (earlier) to bring good luck. It is probable therefore that the distribution of largesse was to servants, and that lines 67–70 refer to a giving game between nobility of different sexes. Waldron (p. 32) and Davis (p. 74) both suggest that the forfeit of kisses may have been part of the game. S. R. T. O. D'Ardenne (Bibliography 7, p. 114) cites a contemporary source describing a tourney and feast at the court of 'The Green Count' (Amadeus VI of Savoy): 'After the contest the ladies again bound the knights (in green silk bonds!) and led them to the castle, where their weapons were taken from them. After dinner the knights received their rewards. They had the right to kiss their ladies and receive presents from them.'

73   They do not sit at the Round Table, which was designed to avoid seating according to rank; the poet describes common custom in a medieval castle.

82   Grey (the translation of the French word 'vaire', which originally meant the fur obtained from a squirrel with a grey back and white belly) was the conventional colour of medieval romance beauties' eyes. Waldron (p. 33) is not alone in suggesting that what we loosely understand by 'blue' may be meant. My own view is that grey means grey: most 'blue-eyed' people have grey eyes tinged with blue, and really blue eyes are very rare.

91   'This custom of Arthur's is mentioned in many French romances . . .' (Davis, p. 76).

110   Agravain was Gawain's brother. Both were sons of King Lot of Orkney and Arthur's half-sister Anna (or Belisent).

112   Guinevere was on Arthur's left (as shown in the first of the illustrations to the poem on the manuscript), and to her left were Gawain and then Agravain. Bishop Baldwin 'began the board' because he was on King Arthur's right, i.e. in the position of honour.

118   The kind of drum specified was the 'nakers', a double military drum slung on the body, which Crusaders brought back from the east. A picture in the National Gallery, London, the *Madonna with the Girdle* by Matteo di Giovanni (c. 1435–95), shows a musical angel playing nakers. Modern bongos are direct descendants of nakers.

128   The company fed and were served in pairs. Thus Gawain and Agravain are one pair, Bishop Baldwin and Ywain another.

133   i.e. It was a noise heralding a challenge of the kind stipulated in ll. 96–9 as necessary before King Arthur could begin the feast.

160   This is a precise, and also the first, indication that the Green Knight is completely unarmoured; knights

commonly wore hose, but not armoured shoes, when not prepared for fighting. This detail would be significant for the fourteenth-century listener.

167   The 'gauds' may be big beads, with a suggestion of our word 'gaudy'.

206   The holly cluster or wassail bob (its living green leaves promising that spring would succeed dead midwinter) was a symbol of Christmas good luck, though its origin as such is pagan. The early Christians in Rome probably took it over from the Saturnalia, in which it figured prominently, Saturn's club being made of holly wood.

209   There is no 'helmet-smasher' in the original text. But we have only one word for the weapon left in our language – axe, repeated use of which would fail to give the accreting sense of the poet's variations. The text word here is 'sparthe', a long-handled, broad-bladed battle-axe. Hence the description of the blade' as being an ell (45 inches) long. 'Helmet-smasher' comes from a suggested etymology for another kind of axe, the halberd, a synonym of which, 'gisarme', is used the next time the weapon is mentioned (l. 288). It is the ironic skill of the poet to delay description of the axe, which would of course strike Arthur's court simultaneously with the greenness of the visitant, until last thing before the action continues. Holly cluster and reins in one hand, axe in the other? Perhaps a supernatural horse does not need to be guided to the dais.

237, 241–2   'Those standing' are presumably the servants, with whose behaviour that of 'the doughty', who are 'sitting stock-still', is contrasted.

256–74   This is the only occasion on which the Green Knight speaks with something like the courtly politeness elsewhere exemplified in the words of Arthur, Gawain and the Hostess. In his next speech, the conventional boast and insult of the Challenge appear, and he rarely thereafter uses the delicate qualifying phrases which distinguish this speech.

304   '... the Green Knight's fierce red eyes, a common feature of angry churls in medieval poetry' (Larry D. Benson, Bibliography 2, p. 11).

336   D. E. Baughan (Bibliography 8, p. 246) and Mother Angela Carson (Bibliography 15, p. 14) both think that Arthur here attempts to strike the Green Knight. He fails because his wife is unchaste – a traditional bar to the successful accomplishment of tests. If they are right – and I don't think it is quite justifiable to import presumed source material like that – then Gawain has a further motive for rescuing Arthur from his predicament, and his tact in the following speech is enhanced.

339   Until this point Gawain has had no part in the story. The exemplary courtesy, humility and ceremony of his first speech usher in the main theme of the poem and its protagonist.

428   This is no meretricious horror. In folklore, if an enchanter has his head chopped off and can be prevented from re-uniting head and body, he really dies. So the kicking is probably purposeful. This enchanter not only regains his head, but demonstrates superior power by riding off with his 'head in his hand'.

445   Gollancz (p. 103) says that the 'fairest in fame' means Guinevere, presumably because (see Waldron, p. 49, who rejects this idea) to terrify Guinevere turns out to be a main motive of the Green Knight's enterprise (ll. 2460–2). But the phrase in the original, 'derrest

on dece' has the ring of alliterative convenience, and in any case the words the head speaks are addressed to Gawain.

460   Waldron (p. 50) notes that this phrase describing the exit of the Green Knight is a 'fairy' formula conventionally applied to supernatural beings. I note that it retained enough vital currency for such a late poet as Spenser to apply it effectively to the departure of Nature at the end of the gods' debate on Mutability in the *Mutabilitie Cantos*:

> Then was that whole assembly quite dismisst (i.e. everyone knows where the gods go after doing business on earth)
> And Natur's selfe did vanish, whither no man wist. (But the ambiguous figure of Nature encourages only uncertainty)

462   Since critics have explained so diversely the behaviour of Arthur and Gawain after the Green Knight's departure, the poet's own explanation (ll. 467–77) must be underlined. The king's laughter and explanation are the calculated actions of a good leader restoring normality and morale to the community after a terrifying and dangerous experience.

477   'Hang up your axe' was a proverbial instruction to cease strife or stop work. Here the double use, for Gawain is literally hanging up his axe as well as completing a job, testifies to Arthur's wit: hence the 'gracefully' in the previous line.

Fit II

500   This beautiful passage on the cycle of the seasons develops a conventional medieval subject, with its contrasts and often very forcible oppositions, as a

device of dramatic suspense to heighten the pathos of the hero's predicament. Lines 498–531 above were set as a choral work by Harrison Birtwistle under the title: *Narration, a description of the passing of a year*, and sung by the John Alldis Choir at the Wigmore Hall, London, on St Valentine's Day, 14 February 1964.

536   All Saints' Day is 1 November. Gawain allows two months for finding the Green Chapel, and prepares for departure on a feast day of traditional rejoicing.

551   Eric is the hero of Chrétien de Troyes' *Erec et Enide* in which (according to Davis) he is described as second in renown of Arthur's knights, after Gawain. Lancelot of the Lake is there rated third.

552   Sir Dodinal (or Doddinaval) 'le Savage' was so called on account of his love of hunting.

The Duke of Clarence, another cousin of Gawain's, being the son of King Nantres and Arthur's half-sister Blasine, is particularly interesting because in the Vulgate *Lancelot* he has an adventure similar to part of Gawain's. While looking for Gawain, who is imprisoned in the Dolorous Tower, he lodges with a vavasour who tries to dissuade him from travelling through a valley from which nobody returns. Even his squire tries to persuade him not to go on, and refuses to follow him into the valley (condensed from Gollancz p. 104).

553   Lancelot, the famous son of King Ban of Benwick, only late in the development of Arthurian romance becomes the lover of Queen Guinevere, and the chief knight at court.

Lionel was the son of King Bohors of Gannes, and Lancelot's cousin.

Lucan, the royal butler, and Gifflet, in the Vulgate *Morte Arthur*, were the last left alive with Arthur after the final battle on Salisbury Plain. In the chapel Arthur, giving him a last embrace, pressed him to death (from Gollancz p. 104).

554   Bors was Lionel's brother.

Bedivere, who in Malory is the last survivor of Arthur's battle with Mordred, was the great friend of Kay. Together they went with Arthur to meet the giant of St Michael's Mount, and later fought prodigiously in Arthur's great victory over the Romans. According to Geoffrey of Monmouth, both were slain in this battle.

555   Mador (de la Port) 'brother of Gaheris de Careheu, who was killed at the Queen's table by poisoned apples intended for Gawain. Mador appealed for justice against the Queen, who could find no knight to defend her until, on the last of her forty days' respite, Lancelot appeared in disguise and saved her life by defeating Mador.' (Gollancz p. 105).

597   'Gringolet' appears as the name of Gawain's horse in Chrétien de Troyes (twelfth century). The word probably derives from 'Gwyngalet', meaning 'white-hard'. Later the name was assigned to the boat of the mythical hero Wade, the son of Wayland the Smith and Bodhilda, the King of Sweden's daughter.

611–12   Davis has a long and fascinating note (pp. 91–2) on the use in medieval decoration – whether in manuscript illumination and adornment, clothing, tapestry or metalwork (he might have added sculpture) – of such features as the periwinkle, turtle-doves and true-love-knots. He thinks the latter means the flowers rather than the devices.

619   One of the five smaller coloured initials marks the

beginning of this section describing Gawain's shield.

620 For the Pentangle, see pp.131 and 147-9.

640 Lamentation for misuse of the five wits was common in penitential exercises in the fourteenth century. John of Gaunt in his will refers to 'mes cynk scens lesquelx j'ay multz negligentment despendie' (my five wits which I have most negligently misspent) – Robert W. Ackerman, (Bibliography 10, p. 264). Although we distinguish between the five senses and the five wits, the senses ('scens' above) were termed 'wits' before the qualities of mind.

646 The number of the joys may vary from five to fifteen. In medieval England they were usually five: the Annunciation, Nativity, Resurrection, Ascension and Assumption.

652 Translating terms defining concepts peculiar to a remote period is a tricky business. The five original terms stated in the poem with possible translations and glosses, are:

fraunchise: liberality, magnanimity, free-hearted generosity appropriate to a noble

felaȝschyp: love of fellow men, lovingkindness

clannes: purity of mind and spirit, chastity, continence

cortaysye: courtesy

pité: piety, compassion

675-83 An interesting variant of a feature often found in romance – regret for an adventure rashly undertaken, or a promise rashly made. The courtiers' reference to arrogance shows that they do not at this stage understand the values that are at stake; and the isolation Gawain accordingly suffers brings him sympathy from audience and reader.

697-701 Gawain comes from an unlocated Camelot to north-western Wales and enters a known region with real names before going again into the unknown. Davis (p. 97) discusses Gawain's itinerary at length: it passes near Holy Well, where Caradoc, Prince of Wales decapitated St Winifred for refusing his advances. Where the head fell, the holy well broke out. St Benno restored her to life, and the white circle round her neck remained as testimony of her fidelity to Christ. Gollancz (p. 107) relates this, and concludes that the story 'would make a natural appeal to Gawain'. But Davis thinks this fanciful, since there is no reference to the story in the poem. In the fourteenth century the wilderness of Wirral had become a refuge for vagabonds and outlaws to such an extent that in July 1376 Edward III, on the petition of the citizens of Chester, ordered the disafforestation of the area.

715–16   Fierce guardians of water-crossings are common adversaries for virtuous knights in medieval romance.

721   The wild man of the woods was a monstrous sub-human creature often met in medieval literature and art. He survived to appear in Spenser's *Faerie Queene* (Book IV, Canto VII) and to be represented several times in the Elizabethan drama; Caliban is one in essence. These wild men specialized in carrying off women and fighting knights.

763   One of the five smaller coloured initials marks this section.

774   Sir Gawain thanks St Julian the Hospitaller, who is the patron saint of travellers and of hospitality.

786   Of the castle which the poet now describes, R. W. V. Elliott (Bibliography 11, p. 75) writes: 'The castle is not the Grail Castle; it is the most "modern" piece of

description in the whole poem. Architectural features which as yet existed only in isolation on fourteenth-century buildings are here assembled to create a remarkable anticipation of a fifteenth-century castle.'

802   There was a custom of decorating food with castles cut out of paper – which is mentioned with disgust by Chaucer's Parson (Robert W. Ackerman, Bibliography 12, pp. 410–17).

813   A nice irony for the porter of this deceptive castle to swear by the keeper of heaven-portal!

843   Parallels have been drawn between this description of Bertilak and that of the Green Knight on his first appearance at Camelot (137 ff.), but the only qualities which appear to me to be common to both men are the conventional ones of size and strength. The Green Knight is hirsute and green, Bertilak's predominant hue is red ('beaver-hued', 'face fierce as fire'). It is in their behaviour and speech that the poet places the correspondences.

866   Gawain is never described in the poem, except by his attributes. His personification of spring here is more likely to be a conventional tribute to his good looks and youth than a deliberate reminder of the solar and spring-like qualities of the hero in the primitive analogues of one part of the story.

888–98   An exchange of formal courtesy on the day of semi-fasting before Christmas. The meatless meal is described, and Gawain nevertheless judges it a feast, whereupon the servers self-deprecatingly call it a penance.

908   Compare the lord's reaction to the news that his guest is Gawain with the similar rejoicing of the Green Knight at l. 390.

916–27   An ironic clash of two sets of expectation. Our expectation concerns a brave Gawain fighting maleficent Nature and the supernatural: that of the knights, a traditional courtly Gawain. They will both be fulfilled in unexpected ways.

943–69   The description of the two ladies is based on a conventional antithesis between youth and age. The discerning among the audience might harbour a neo-Platonic suspicion that from an old lady so ugly, not only good might be expected. The exposed beauty of the young lady, and the swathed ugliness of the old one, are faithful to a tradition in painting which personified virtue and innocence naked, but vice and shame draped.

992   The manuscript reads 'kyng', but editors amend to 'lord', which not only makes the alliterative pattern correct, but is the term mostly used to describe the lord of the castle. However, Larry D. Benson (Bibliography 4, p. 80), considering the extent to which the Green Knight may be a wild man of the woods, writes 'the wild man is of course a king of the wilderness', and thinks that the emendation is unnecessary.

1003   The formal pairing at table of Gawain and his hostess would appear significant to listeners familiar with folk-tales and romances in which kings offered their wives to guests, usually to test them or gain power over them. Behind this tradition lies the primitive hospitality of wife-sharing with a guest, which is still observed in some societies.

1021   St John's Day is 27 December, and since the last three days of the year are accounted for by the hunting and wooing sequences, the 28 December, Holy Innocent's Day, is missing. Gollancz (pp. 110–11) suggests that a line which refers to it may have been lost in transcription.

1047   'Fierce exploit': there is an ambiguity here which the reader who knows that the 'exploit' lies in the future may miss. Waldron (p. 75) suggests a possible humorous interpretation which well suits the lord's temperament: 'What crime had you committed that you had to leave Arthur's court so hurriedly?' (i.e. during the Christmas season).

1054   'Logres' meant 'approximately England south of the Humber' (Davis, p. 98), and was so named after Locrine, one of the legendary kings of Britain. There is an absurd Elizabethan *Tragedie of Locrine discoursing the Warres of the Britaines and the Hunnes,* which was printed in the Third Shakespeare Folio of 1664.

1071   'Slepynge longe in greet quiete is eek a greet norrice to Leccherie', according to Chaucer's Parson, as Benson points out (Bibliography 4, p. 108).

1105   The Exchange of Winnings theme enters – *after* the lord of the castle has first bound Gawain by promise to lie long in bed and take his meal with his hostess. Promise-making and promise-extracting have a double effect. They make for suspense, because the listener waits for the expected trap to be sprung, and they are structural in a poem in which the hero's good faith is the main concern.

Fit III

1141   The fourteenth-century hunting horn had only one note; a combination of shorts and longs was used for making different calls, which were transcribed as *mote, trut, trororout, trorororout.*

1157	The close season for male deer ('harts' and 'brave bucks') was 14 September to 24 June, but female deer were hunted from 14 September to 2 February.
1179	The Temptation theme enters.
1237	Davis (pp. 108–9) follows older critics like Gollancz and Gwyn Jones, and makes a great fuss of his determination to clear the Lady of the charge of bluntly offering Gawain her body, but the context, 'Do with it what you will', following upon such actions of the Lady as securing the door and holding him down in the bed, removes any doubt about what she is up to. See further discussion on pp. 119–21, 132–5.
1276	Gawain clinches his win in this first round by tactfully reminding the Lady that she is married. That said, he can safely offer her chaste knightly service.
1283	I follow Gollancz and Waldron in accepting an emendation of Morris which gives the thought in this line to Gawain rather than to the Lady. The MS reading not only offers a clumsy anacoluthon and an alliterating word ('burde') twice in a line, but introduces a narrative technique, that of suddenly entering the Lady's mind, where it is inappropriate. I take the manuscript to be corrupt at this point.
1325	Davis (p. 111) notes that, as elsewhere in Romance, 'the nobles and gentry made it a point of honour to be skilled in breaking up deer'.
1347	Strictly speaking, the numbles is offal from the back and loins.
1355	The raven's fee: a piece of gristle on the end of the breast-bone was always flung to the ravens and crows which gathered at a hunt – to propitiate dark powers?
1388–94	Gawain's good faith is maintained as he balances on a knife-edge. He gives his host the kind of hug and kiss that he received from the Lady, and takes a

stand on the letter of his promise in order not to reveal anything that could bring discredit on either her or himself.

1412   For medieval belief about cocks crowing at night, see note to l. 2008.

1421   One of the five smaller coloured initials marks this line on the manuscript.

1423   According to Turberville (*The Noble Art of Venerie, or Hunting*, 1573) hounds engaged in boar-hunting needed special encouragement: 'You shall comfort your houndes with furious terrible soundes and noyse as well of the voyce as also of your horne' (Gollancz, p. 116).

1457   The bristles of the brow grow more thickly when the boar has its winter coat. When at bay, with its flanks and rear protected, the boar could be fatally hit only by a shot between the eyes.

1550   Davis (p. 116) suggests that ME 'woze', which editors generally take to be a noun meaning 'wrong', might be the infinitive 'to woo'. In either case, here for the first time the poet hints that the motive of the Hostess may not be love or lust.

1584   To kill a boar with a sword rather than a spear, and without the help of hounds, was considered especially noble.

1626   The shields are 'the thick tough skin upon the sides and flanks of the boar' (Shorter OED).

1644   St Giles, a hermit who lived in a forest near Nîmes, and the patron saint of cripples, has as his symbol a hind. The tradition is that during a hunt he was accidentally hit in the knee by an arrow shot by Childeric, a seventh-century king of France.

1647   The Host's point being that Gawain has doubled the previous day's takings.

1655	The Christmas carol (ME 'coundute') was a song for tenor with two descants, which apparently originated in 'a motet sung while the priest was proceeding to the altar' (Davis, p. 118).
1679	How did Gawain understand this judgement of his host? Especially when it was followed by the ominous 'Think of that tomorrow!' and the gloomy reminder of fate.
1699	Although accounts of the hunting of deer and boar are common in medieval romance, descriptions of fox-hunting are rare. It was certainly a less noble sport, and the Host's attitude to his quarry (l. 1944) accords with the general view of the fox as being little better than vermin.
1702	Turberville recommends the putting of vinegar into the nostrils of a hound 'for to make him snuffe, to the end his scent may be perfecter'! (Gollancz, p. 120)
1733 ff.	A beautiful piece of narration, this. The Lady could not sleep 'for luf'. My translation takes account of the ambiguity of the word, which was used in the general sense of liking as well as love and was certainly appropriate to describe the aesthetic pleasure derived from 'luf-talkynge', the ecstatic but mainly verbal dalliance of the practitioners of courtly love. But then, in the next line, comes 'the purpose pitched in her heart' – a mysterious alarm to the listener who is, however, swiftly lulled back to a conventional interpretation of the Lady's motive by the description of her beauty, with its emphasis on her décolletage (l. 1741), a standard weapon in the wars of courtly love. The contrast between her brisk opening of the window and the ominous phantasmagoria of Gawain's dreams (ll. 1743–53) completes the setting for the third temptation scene.

1762   The nearest the poet gets to suggesting that Gawain's sexual impulse was actually stirred – and it's not very near. He is describing the virtually Platonic ecstasy of 'luf-talkynge' with a beautiful and witty woman.

1770–75   The most complete statement of Gawain's multiple predicament, which some critics have mistakenly considered to be the necessity to defend a *single* virtue, such as chastity or courtesy.

1788   Gawain swears by St John, presumably the Evangelist whose day, 27 December, has just passed. Waldron (p. 106) notes that St John was 'by tradition supremely devoted to celibacy'.

1849   The magic girdle is found elsewhere in Romance. In Diu Krône, Gawain gives to Guinevere, who in turn gives to Gasozein, a girdle which makes the wearer invincible in battle and also brings him the love of men and women. Waldron, whose glosses on weight of meaning are always illuminating, notes (p. 109) that the very strong slaughter word (ME 'tohewe') which I have translated as 'hack to pieces' 'is calculated to make Gawain think of his own plight just as "slyght" [my translation of which is 'cunning'] . . . seems designed to suggest that the girdle may be a match for the Green Knight's magical powers.'

1864   Although Gawain swears to conceal the gift of the girdle, it seems that when he dresses for his ordeal (ll. 2030–36) it is visible, and it is a fair inference from line 2358 that the Green Knight can see it.

1876   Gawain goes to chapel after each of the three encounters with his hostess, but this time it is not to mass, but to confession.

1883   Critics disagree about the propriety of Gawain's being 'absolved with certainty' though keeping the girdle, and yet at the end confessing (l. 2374) to 'cowardice and covetousness' on account of keeping it. Davis (p. 123) thinks 'The poet evidently did not regard the retention of the girdle as one of Gawain's "Mysdedes"... which required to be confessed', but I prefer the view of Donald R. Howard (Bibliography 13, p. 229) that 'Gawain is guilty not because he desires to "sauen hymself", but because in order to do so he uses worldly means in the wrong way.' For further discussion, see p. 135–6.

1893   One of the five smaller coloured initials marks this line on the manuscript.

1928   Gawain wears the colour of faithfulness, blue, to perpetrate his one deception!

1934   Gawain's taking of the initiative in making the exchange on this occasion, and his haste to end the discussion, mark his deception (in not giving the Host the girdle) with psychological acuity.

1951   For discussion of the relation between the hunting and wooing scenes, see Introduction, pp. 16–18.

1970   Another masterly piece of combined suspense and innuendo. The Host's remark looks forward to the next step in the Beheading Game, and back to Gawain's very recent failure to perform *his* promise.

Fit IV

2008   Cocks were thought to crow exactly on the hour during the night, and especially at midnight, 3 a.m., and an hour before the dawn (see Waldron p. 115).

2018   One method of ridding armour of rust was to put it into a barrel of sand and roll it about.

2061   This man is of course not Gawain's squire, as he rode out from Camelot alone, but the guide supplied by the Host.

2074 More than one commentator has suggested that this servant is the Green Knight in yet another shape, because in the analogues the Tempter or Antagonist often assumes an unexpected shape to subject the hero to an extra ordeal. But more important than that suggestion, which receives no explicit support from the text, is the fact that the speech habits of this guide – the frequent imperatives, the blunt and even colloquial language – are like those of the Green Knight. Moreover, he handles his horse (ll. 2152–4) in the same violently churlish manner as the Green Knight (l. 457). Contrast with Gawain's courtly handling of his horse (ll. 670 and 2062–3).

2106–9 i.e. He does not operate by the laws of chivalry, which protected churchmen, and did not count fighting with churls as chivalrous.

2137 The word in the original is 'staue', meaning a staff or club, but Gollancz translates 'axe', without linguistic warrant that I can discover. A club is the sort of weapon one would expect to find used by the haunter of a fairy mound, and Davis cites from the Mabinogion an example of a black man on a mound who wields one. But why Gawain should expect to meet anyone but the Green Knight with his axe is not clear.

2162 Various locations have been suggested for the eerie setting of Gawain's last trial. The Peak District and the Staffordshire moorlands have been mooted, as these are the nearest high regions to the Wirral, the last known place named in Gawain's journey. According to R. W. V. Elliott, writing in *The Times* of 21 May 1958, the poet may have had in mind the district of Swythamley Park in Staffordshire, and the craggy feature of the Roaches in particular. Following

Mr Elliott's suggestion, I walked the area, and found the scenery like that described in the poem, complete with legend-haunted natural chapel.

2180 ff. As the poet describes it, the Green Chapel is exactly like an entrance to the Celtic Other World. But Gawain as a Christian sees it as an entrance to hell.

2201 Only one of the parallel romances mentions the whetting, and then only briefly.

2223 This Danish axe, so called because the Vikings used it, was, according to the OED, 'a kind of battle-axe with a very long blade, and usually without a spike on the back'. The weapon the Green Knight had at Arthur's court was a guisarm, or battle-axe complete with spike.

2226 I follow Waldron rather than Davis, in finding it apter for the poet, seeing the Green Knight from Gawain's point of view, to swear to the length of the blade by the girdle, than to offer as a measure an axe-thong or lace which has nowhere been mentioned.

2259 One of the five smaller coloured initials marks this line on the manuscript.

2284 Waldron thinks (p. 127) that 'bring me to the point' is a play on words, and refers to line 2392.

2316 Evidently a standing jump is the quickest way for Gawain to put himself far enough away from the Green Knight to adjust his armour for fighting.

2335 The shift in the Green Knight's sensibility prepares for his shift of function – from Tempter to Confessor.

2368 Indeed 'love of life' is 'less blameworthy' than desire of riches or love, but as Howard (Bibliography 13, p. 240) points out, 'the tiniest peccadillo, however insignificant it may seem, leads to others' –

in this case, to deceiving one's host, and to illicitly and one-sidedly varying the conditions of a compact.

2370   Gawain's first loss of composure; his fierce gibe at his adversary's delay in dealing the return blow (l. 2300) is according to the common convention of duelling of all kinds. And shame and guilt are good grounds for loss of composure.

2414   This outburst reads like a stock medieval anti-feminist tirade from a homily. But it has to be seen in the context of Gawain's confession and expiation, and measured against his own high standards of behaviour.

2445   Bertilak de Hautdesert. The name Bertilak, Davis says (p. 128) is 'apparently of Celtic origin' (see Introduction, p. 12). Hautdesert must be the name of the castle. Waldron, noting that 'desert' in Celtic had come to mean 'hermitage', thinks that the name reinforces Bertilak's confessional function, but J. A. Burrow (Bibliography 14, p. 125) points out that 'at least two medieval English castles, one in Warwickshire, the other in Staffordshire, were called "Beaudesert"' ... so there is no need to go to Celtic 'disert' ('hermitage') to explain the second element. Davis concurs, noting that 'desert' was 'an extremely common element in French place-names'.

2446   Morgan the Fay. See pp. 119–21 and 151–3.

2448   Merlin. See p. 154–5.

2478   The Green Knight's dismissal by the poet assures me that he does not simply revert to a human life as Bertilak, the lord of a castle. See Introduction, pp. 18–19.

2487   'Under the left arm' because the 'tarnishing sin' was *sinister*?

2516   The conjunction of the green baldric and the motto of the Order of the Garter ('added at the end, possibly by a later scribe' – Gollancz p. 132) has been taken to mean that the poem was written for the institution of the Garter; but that order was founded by Edward III in about 1347, and its distinctive badge was a garter of dark blue velvet. The ballad of the Green Knight, which dates from much later, and seems rather debasedly to be based on this poem, deliberately associates the Order of the Bath with this story. Ritual purification of knights by bathing seems to have been practised in England as long ago as the eleventh century, and the Order was formally constituted for the coronation of Henry IV in 1399. But no insignia were worn by the holders. When revived four hundred years later, the Order of the Bath had a crimson ribbon; no trace of green is found anywhere, although Froissart, as quoted by Seldon (1672), refers to a silk ribbon.

PENGUIN ONLINE